The Scent of Mogra and Other Stories

APARNA KAJI SHAH

inanna poetry & fiction series

INANNA PUBLICATIONS AND EDUCATION INC.
TORONTO, CANADA

Canada Council   Conseil des Arts   ONTARIO ARTS COUNCIL   Canada
for the Arts   du Canada   CONSEIL DES ARTS DE L'ONTARIO
                                      an Ontario government agency
                                      un organisme du gouvernement de l'Ontario

We gratefully acknowledge the support of the Canada Council for the Arts and the Ontario Arts Council for our publishing program. We also acknowledge the financial support of the Government of Canada.

Cover design: Val Fullard

Library and Archives Canada Cataloguing in Publication

Shah, Aparna Kaji, author
          The scent of Mogra, and other stories / Aparna Kaji Shah.

(Inanna poetry & fiction series)
Issued in print and electronic formats.
ISBN 978-1-77133-561-4 (softcover).--ISBN 978-1-77133-562-1 (epub).--
ISBN 978-1-77133-563-8 (Kindle).--ISBN 978-1-77133-564-5 (pdf)

          I. Title. II. Series: Inanna poetry and fiction series

PS8637.H348S34 2018   C813'.6   C2018-904370-9
                                             C2018-904371-7

Printed and bound in Canada

FSC
www.fsc.org

MIX
Paper from
responsible sources
FSC® C004071

Inanna Publications and Education Inc.
210 Founders College, York University
4700 Keele Street, Toronto, Ontario M3J 1P3 Canada
Telephone: (416) 736-5356   Fax (416) 736-5765
Email: inanna.publications@inanna.ca Website: www.inanna.ca

For my mother,
Who nurtured me by being herself.

Table of Contents

Maya

❦

AYA'S EYES WIDENED when she entered the gallery. She was stuck at the entrance, clutching the doorframe, as she looked at what was before her. Every inch of the walls was covered with sunshine. The central wall was undulating, with its valleys and peaks painted in different shades of yellow. Her shining brown eyes moved to the wall on her left, her gaze fixed on the glowing murals beckoning her to come in and lose herself in their richness.

"Excuse me, Ma'am," a young man's voice behind her said. Startled, she jerked forward into the gallery as if drawn by a magnet. Now she stood close to the creamy wall, and like a fly in a bowl of custard she was sucked down. She remembered the taste of custard that her mother used to make and serve with red jelly, and she salivated. She imagined biting into a juicy grape swimming in the stuff, and its tartness brought her back to where she was; inside her friend's gallery.

She turned toward the wall on her right, deliberately ignoring the central wall she had been so mesmerized by earlier. The right wall stilled her mind for a moment, as she focused on its rough, corrugated surface. It too was painted yellow, but tinted with greens, browns, and shades of grey/black. She was distracted by a couple of teenagers who were chattering away and giggling, but they soon left. She thought she was alone in the room, till she noticed the young man she had blocked at the entrance. He was at the far corner, quietly taking notes as

1

he stood before the central mural. An art student, perhaps?

Again, she gazed at the art. She stepped back to get a better look, tucking her shoulder-length brown hair behind her ears, so that it didn't fall over her eyes. It's a forest, she thought. The brown strokes are the tree trunks, the green leaves, thick and lush. The yellow was sunlight peering through dense foliage. A dark gloomy forest, shrouded with mist in the early morning, the sun trying to penetrate the vegetation as the day progressed. What if she got lost in this jungle? How would she ever find her way back? She shivered, imagining dusk as it fell, lengthening the shadows of the trees on the forest floor.

The young man's movements attracted her attention away from the painted wall. He looked at her, and she saw that he was not that young after all. He had chiselled features, and a mop of unkept dark hair. His almond-shaped eyes looked at her inquiringly as he scratched his unshaven chin. She returned his gaze, and their eyes locked briefly. She turned back to the wall, and was once again lost in the forest, with this man guiding her by the arm. They rested against a tree trunk. The birds called out as they found a place to rest during dark night, which was rapidly descending upon them. She looked at the man, and he, holding her hand, looked deep into her eyes. Without a word, they both slid down on the forest floor and turned towards each other, her breasts almost, but not quite, touching his chest.

"Excuse me." The man's voice startled her again. She whirled around to face him, and as she did so her *dupatta* slid down her shoulders and fell to the floor. They both bent down to pick it up. He got there first, and as they straightened up, their faces close to each other, they laughed. She embarrassed, he with delight, as he admired the orange-yellow colour of the fabric. When she stretched out her slim pale hand to take it from him, he grinned at her, and put the *dupatta* against his *kurta,* which was a pale yellow. Then he returned the *dupatta* to her. They stood there smiling at each other, and she imagined lying down with him on the forest floor.

He said, "You have spent a long time looking at these paintings. Are you an artist?"

"Oh no," she said. "I ... my friend owns this gallery. I stop by sometimes. Yellow is my favourite colour." *He is about ten years younger than me*, she thought. "Are *you* an artist?"

"Look, there is a nice little café behind this gallery. I was planning to go there. Why don't we go there and chat? My name is Rahul." Maya saw that the gallery was filling up, and they would be disturbing the viewers by talking. Her throat was parched, and she was longing for a cup of tea.

"Okay, why not?" she smiled, then added, "I'm Maya."

They made their way out the door, and went around the building to the café entrance. He is tall, she thought as she glanced at him sideways. His body was muscular and lean, as if he worked out every day. Her own body, though still slim, was soft like ripe fruit, her arms sagging a little. Thank god, they were covered by three-quarter sleeves.

The café was quiet. They chose a table close to a wall. Maya noticed that it was painted a pastel yellow, though it looked almost cream-coloured in the dim lighting. A few framed black-and-white photographs hung on the wall, photographs of Bombay of an earlier era. Now, Bombay was very different. It was Mumbai.

Here she was with this strange man, when by now she should have been at her mother's place. Her phone vibrated, and she told her mother that she was delayed and would be there soon. They ordered tea and sandwiches. She let out a sigh and Rahul raised his eyebrows, while a crooked smile lifted the left corner of his lips.

"Well, this is unplanned," Maya said, "and I have a lot of things to do this evening."

"Some of the best things are spontaneous, don't you think?"

She nodded, and her mind took her to a different time and a

different place. The library was locked. It was only five o'clock, and she had an assignment due the next day. She knocked on the door, and waited in vain. Another student ran up the stairs behind her. He said, "How can the library be closed? Exams begin next week. Well, I'm going to find an empty classroom to study. Would you like to come with me?"

They both ran down the stairs, and found a science classroom that was empty since the students were in the lab. They introduced themselves to each other. She was a psychology major, and he was studying economics. His name was Rakesh. Maya and Rakesh worked until the science students came back. They decided to get a bite to eat before going home. Her mother was upset when Maya told her, admonishing her that it was not a good idea to go out with strange men.

And now she was doing it again. Maya was forty-nine, and Rahul was probably just under forty. Then, she was a young nineteen-year-old. Rakesh had proposed to her when they both graduated, but she wanted to go to study in the U.S., while he had to find a job right away. They had corresponded for a while, but the relationship petered out within a year. When she had sought him out after three years of post-graduate work, he was already married.

Her mother had introduced her to many young men, but nothing had clicked. Her mother was worried. She was well into her seventies, and wouldn't be there forever. And now it was too late. Or was it?

"Would you like another cup of tea?" Rahul said.

"Oh no. I should get going soon. I need to go and see my mother, then get home to do some class prep. I have an early morning class tomorrow."

"Psychology, you told me. I was always interested in the subject. Also, there is so much to learn about the creative process from psychology. Maybe another time, you could tell me about that." He paused, trying to gauge her reaction to "another time." Would there be another time? She didn't know.

He spoke again. "Where is home?"

"Colaba. What about you?"

"I live at Tardeo. I share an apartment with a friend. He teaches at the J.J School of Art. Where do you teach?"

"Sophia College." She picked up her bag, and started to take out money for her share of the tea and sandwiches. He touched her hand to restrain her.

"I invited you to join me. The next time you can pay." He smiled. "Can we meet again? Here is my number." He gave her a business card. Rahul Saxena.

"Thanks," she smiled. "Sorry, I don't have a card. I'll try to call you," she said and then left. Call and do what? she thought. Just see what this encounter leads to, if anything? She wouldn't call, she knew. It always led to disillusion and disappointment, for her at least. Some of her friends were lucky that such meetings ended up in a long-term commitment, or marriage.

She was relieved that her mother looked more cheerful than the last time she had visited her. Maya knew that she had been lonely ever since her father died almost two years ago. She had started clinging to Maya, the only child who lived in Mumbai; Maya's brother lived in Canada. Her mother was financially comfortable, but was dependent on Maya emotionally. Maya made sure that her mother was doing well, but she saw her no more than once a week.

It was close to seven in the evening when she finally reached home. Her mother had given her some *parathas* and a curry, but she was still full from her tea and sandwiches. Rahul. What is he doing now? she caught herself wondering. Who cares? She wasn't going to call him anyway. He had told her that he was in the middle of painting three figures in the foreground of a huge canvas, with a stark landscape as the background. When she asked who the three figures were, he had smiled and shaken his head.

She had to finish marking assignments for the next day, and be in bed by eleven, if she was going to make it to her eight o'clock class rested and prepared. That night she dreamt of the dark forest in the wall mural, and that she was lying down on the forest floor under a tree, with a man lying down next to her.

No, she was not a virgin. During the three years that she had lived in the U.S. she had remained a virgin, subconsciously "keeping" herself for Rakesh. But after she had discovered that he was already married, she had plunged into a relationship right away. She thought it a serious relationship and she had agreed to sex. They had talked about books, enjoyed movies together, and he had even cooked for her at her place. But it had all turned to ashes when she accidently found out that he was also intimately involved with another woman.

Tomorrow was her friend Usha's anniversary party. Maya remembered her wedding as if it was just yesterday. At the time, Maya had been recovering from yet another affair that had turned sour. What was the reason that relationship had ended? Oh, right, she had not been enough of an intellectual for him. He was an Economics professor at her college. The sex they had was cold and mechanical, something to be gotten over with quickly for the release it provided, so that they could resume discussing the latest economic reform in the country. She was still smarting from the humiliation of not being cerebral enough for him. Yet, she had enjoyed Usha's wedding. She and her friends had together decided what to wear for each event. Her friends had even encouraged her to buy the latest fashions, hoping to set her up with their husbands' unmarried cousins and brothers.

The wedding had led to another relationship, which had lasted almost a full year. But Satish was a lawyer, and too busy to commit. Their relationship had died a natural death. That was nine years ago. She had just turned forty, and Satish was forty-six, previously married and divorced.

Luckily, she found a seat on the crowded bus while returning home the next evening. She had to shower and change before going to the anniversary celebration. She looked out the window as the bus passed Marine Drive, and saw couples sitting on the concrete ledge overlooking the sea, deep in conversation with one another, some just holding hands and others strolling along.

Something tugged at her heart strings, and her thoughts turned to the man she had recently met. She knew nothing about him. He seemed to want to get to know her. Didn't he see that she was at least eight to ten years older than him? Why did she think that it was romance that he wanted? Perhaps all he wanted was to discuss the creative process, because she was a psychology professor and interested in art. As she turned the key in her front door, she decided that she would give him a call after all. He was interesting, and what was wrong with simply enjoying some good company?

***

Rahul stretched out his hand and pulled her up, so that she could stand on the ledge of a black rock on which he and Mukul were resting. They had started climbing at nine o'clock, and now it was almost one in the afternoon. She had wanted to rest and eat her sandwiches. They would reach the top of the *ghat* in a couple of hours, rest overnight in Khandala, and return to Mumbai tomorrow. An overnight excursion with two men. Her mother was none too happy, but she loved hiking and mountain climbing, and hadn't done it for over fifteen years. She had been part of the mountaineering club as a student at St. Xavier's.

It was almost ten months since she had first met Rahul at the art gallery, and she had called him a couple of weeks later. They had met for lunch one afternoon after her classes. They had discussed the creative process , told each other about their families, and their upbringing, among myriad other issues of the day. He had called her again, to visit another art galley together, and so it went on. She had had dinner at his place, had met Mukul, Rahul's flat mate. Sometimes they met as a threesome. Mukul was into mountaineering in a big way, and so when she expressed her interest, the two men had persuaded her to join them during the Christmas break at college.

Her friends asked her about her relationship with Rahul, hinting that it may be more than just friendship. She'd shrugged her shoulders, and replied that nothing had happened yet. Occasionally, she did feel the urge to hold his hand when they went to a movie together, but she desisted, and was disappointed that he never made the first move. Gradually, she got used to their platonic relationship, and did not expect anything else. She enjoyed his company, without the pressure that one always felt in a romantic relationship. It was an easy camaraderie, sometimes with teasing and bantering, at other times with serious conversations about art, politics, and social issues.

Her mother asked to meet him, and kept asking her when they would get married. She told her that it wasn't that kind of a relationship, and that she would invite him to meet her only if she promised not to broach the topic of marriage; it would be embarrassing for Rahul and for Maya, and could jeopardize their wonderful friendship. In fact, the three of them were going to have dinner at her mother's place when they returned to Mumbai after their hiking excursion.

* * *

Mukul was getting married. Rahul would have to move out of the Tardeo place, as that is where Mukul and Radhika were going to live. Maya befriended the younger woman, hoping that they could meet as a foursome.

When the question of where Rahul was going to live came up, Maya wanted to offer her place, as she had an extra room, which she used as an office. There was a sofa bed, which could be made up, until Rahul found accommodation. She hesitated. What would everyone think? Would Rahul think of it as a come on? What if it became a permanent arrangement? No, she wouldn't want that; she liked her independence, and did not make the offer.

Finally, Rahul decided to share a flat with a young woman who worked in a bank. It was close to Mukul's place.

Maya spoke up before the final decision was made. She told him how she had thought of offering her place, but had kept quiet because of what everyone would think. In any case, it could not be a permanent arrangement, but if he wanted to look for something else and someone else he could share with, he was welcome to stay temporarily at her flat. Maya had felt a tiny prick of jealousy. She wasn't happy about Rahul sharing an apartment with a woman, and that the woman was much younger than she was. According to Rahul, this woman was attractive as well.

Rahul realized what Maya's feelings were, and he took her out for coffee one evening before his move. "Maya, I don't want to move in with you because I don't want anything to happen to our friendship. Who knows how our relationship might change if we live together. And, in any case, I would still have to find another apartment, and thus have to move twice."

"I understand that. It's just that you don't know this person, the young woman...." Maya said.

"Well, I wouldn't necessarily know the person I might find to share a living space with, whether it was a man or a woman." He stretched out his hand, and covered Maya's, which lay immobile on the table. "Maya, tell me honestly, are you uncomfortable because it is a young woman? Are you jealous?"

She couldn't look him straight in the eye, though he tried to hold hers. As she looked away, she was embarrassed that her eyes were filling up. She tried surreptitiously to wipe away her tears with her *dupatta*, but Rahul knew. He waited for her to recover, and smiled at her when she turned back to look at him. "Are you afraid that I will get involved with Chaya? That I will cozy up with her every evening when she returns from work, and won't want to meet you anymore?"

Maya shook her head. "I know, I'm being silly. Our relationship, our friendship, is our own. And anyway, it's not ...

a romantic relationship." She blushed.

Rahul looked at her steadily, and with affection. "Yes, Maya, it is not ... so far. Things can change...." There was a twinkle in his eye as he said that. "Or you may meet someone you want to marry, or I may meet someone too."

Maya felt much better after that conversation, and helped him pack up and move.

* * *

The phone call she had always dreaded finally came. She was called to the college office during the middle of a lecture. Her mother had fallen, slipped in the bathroom. The maid attending her could not lift her up. Maya rushed over.

In the taxi, she called Rahul to come and help. He reached before she did, and had already called the doctor. Her mother had a weak heart and was probably dizzy. Rahul offered to stay with her for a few hours every day, while Maya finished the college term. He had developed a regard for her mother; his own parents had passed away when he was a teenager.

Maya shifted to her mother's place, so that she would not be alone with the maid at night. It would soon be summer vacation, and Maya would then be able to devote herself to her mother's care. The reality that her mother was getting more and more frail, and would not be there forever, suddenly sunk in.

Maya's brother Nimesh, and his Canadian wife Naomi, came to Mumbai from Toronto for a couple of weeks. Maya had not seen them for over two years. They had exchanged occasional emails, but nothing more than that. Nimesh was the same age as Rahul. During her brother's formative years, Maya had been away, studying in the U.S., so they were not very close. But her mother was thrilled to be with her son, and it gave Maya a little time to herself.

Maya's mother passed away a month later. Maya was still living with her when it happened. Rahul rushed to her side when Maya called him, and held her while she sobbed on his shoulder. It was only after that, that they called everyone who needed to be called and started making funeral arrangements. Nimesh said that he could not come right away, and that she should light the funeral pyre without him. The next few days were a blur for Maya. She did what she was told to do by the elders mechanically. Rahul was always by her side, helping in any way he could.

Life limped back to normal, a new normal for Maya. The summer vacation was over, and she was getting ready for another year at college. Her parents' apartment was now hers. It was a three bedroom on Nepean Sea road, overlooking the sea. She gave up her rented place and permanently moved into her mother's flat. It was much easier to get to Sophia College from there, compared to the apartment she'd rented in Colaba. She was also closer to Rahul and Mukul. The apartment was too large for a single person, but she soon got used to it, and began to enjoy the extra space.

A few months after she had moved in, Nimesh and Naomi came to visit her for three weeks, this time with their sixteen-year-old daughter, Lisa. It was a time of great joy for Maya. Her relationship with her brother and sister-in-law had changed after her mother died. Her mother had never fully accepted Naomi, so she and her brother were always on edge. Now there was a warmth and informality that had never surfaced before. Lisa and she hit it off as well. Maya took her niece shopping, and they often went to movies together. Rahul joined them once or twice, and Lisa was fascinated with this "real" artist; she was thinking of becoming an artist too.

Nimesh told her one evening that they had come down mainly to ensure that she was doing okay, now that their mother was no more. Was there anything that they could do for her? They had met Rahul a few times when Maya had invited him over for dinner with the family. They asked Maya about him. Though they tried not to probe, they wanted to know if she was in a serious relationship with Rahul. When she emphatically told them that she was not, they asked if she would like to move to Canada. She could find a teaching job there, or even a job as a counsellor, if she took couple of courses. Maya, who had never thought of leaving Mumbai, was taken aback, but touched by their concern. She said no right away. But before they left, she told them that she would give it some thought.

As time passed, the idea of moving to Canada took a hold of Maya's mind. A couple of months after Nimesh had left, she spoke to Rahul and her friend Usha about it. Usha encouraged her to think about it seriously. But when she mentioned it to Rahul, he was upset. He said, "Just because your brother has invited you to Toronto, you are thinking of packing up and leaving for good? What about your life here? Your friends, family and career? Granted your mother is no more, but you have a lot of other connections. How can you just forget about all of them ?"

She said, "Yes, I have a whole network of connections here that I would miss. But I'm getting older. Over there I would have my brother, and a sister-in-law, and Lisa."

Rahul said, "Do you think they would do more for you than your closest friends here? And what about adjusting to a new and different lifestyle? You would have to start by upgrading your qualifications. At Sophia College, you could be the head of your department in a couple of years."

That night in bed, she wondered about Rahul's reaction. Did he not want her to leave? But their relationship had not progressed to another level; they were still just close friends. It was true that she had become dependent on his help and support whenever there was a crisis, like her mother's death, but their relationship had never deepened as she had at times hoped it would.

Maya was now excited about the possibility of a new life, in another country. A few weeks later she spoke about it again with Rahul. This time he was calmer, and it seemed he under-stood her point of view. Could she broach the topic of their relationship with him? If it became a permanent commitment, and Maya thought she was ready for it, she would not think of going to Toronto at all. But how was she to begin?

The sun was about to set, and Maya and Rahul were walking along Marine Drive, looking out at the rough monsoon ocean. Maya said, "Rahul, we spend so much time together; how do you feel about our relationship?"

"I feel close to you, and enjoy our time together, he answered quietly.

She paused a moment. "I feel we are like an old couple. We see movies and plays together, we go for walks. Sometimes you accompany me to college events. Your friends as well as mine, often invite us together."

Rahul smiled. "I'm nine years your junior, so we can't be an old couple."

Maya laughed. Then she said, "Seriously, Rahul. Where is this going?"

"Does it have to go anywhere? Why don't we just enjoy what we have without any complications?"

Maya said, "I'm not getting any younger. I've passed the fifty mark. At this stage, I would like something permanent, some commitment."

They were now sitting on the concrete ledge, the waves crashing against it. Rahul looked out at the sea. Maya looked at him, but his expression was inscrutable. She grabbed his arm and said, "What do you think, Rahul?"

"If you mean marriage, I don't know what to say."

"Why don't you ask Mukul and Radhika? They seem very happy. You have other married friends as well."

"What do I need to ask? I know they are happy. But I don't know if I'm made for marriage. There's a finality about it that I'm not comfortable with."

"If we were to settle down together, I wouldn't even think of going to Canada," Maya said.

"That is something that you have to decide."

That was the end of the conversation, and when they took the bus home, they were both busy with their own thoughts, and hardly spoke. When Maya's stop arrived, she said a quick goodbye and alighted. Rahul looked out the window and waved at her. She did not wave back.

In bed that night, many questions raced through Maya's head. *Does he not find me attractive enough? After all, I'm a fifty-year-old woman. Maybe he finds me physically repulsive. His body looks lean and firm at forty-two, but mine is soft, and beginning to droop. And of course, there is more grey in my hair than in his. Or, as he said, he simply does not want the finality of marriage. And it has nothing to do with me or my body.* With that thought, Maya finally fell asleep. She dreamt again of the forest in the painting she had seen so long ago; once again, she and Rahul were sliding down the tree trunk to lie down together on the forest floor.

* * *

They had reached the airport early, worried about road closures and traffic. Rahul had helped her with her two large suitcases. Usha and a cousin had come to see her off as well, though she was only going to be away for six months; she wanted to see if she would like living in Toronto. She had reached that decision a couple of weeks after her conversation with Rahul at Marine Drive. He was not willing to commit to anything. She was not sure if it was a good idea to move to Canada, so this decision kept her options open. Her college had agreed to an extended leave of absence since Maya had found a substitute teacher for her courses. She was going to stay with her brother for a couple of weeks, until they found an apartment for her that she could rent short-term.

On her last evening, she and Rahul had dinner together. There had been so many farewells for her, and it had been a long time since they had been alone. Rahul had finally said something about his feelings. "Maya, I do care for you a lot, and I will miss you terribly. But, I don't … can't think of marriage…." he'd said, his voice a bit shaky.

"Are you shy about sex?" she asked, eyeing him curiously.

He looked down at his plate. "No … I don't know…. I can't see myself as a husband…."

"Have you ever been in a physical relationship?"

"Briefly, yes…. many years ago. But it's not that. It's the finality, the commitment."

"If we get married, everything can remain the same. We can share a bed, but that doesn't have to mean sex," she said.

"You go to Canada, and see what you feel, whether you would like to move there or not. The time away from each other will help us think things through."

She spent a very happy two weeks at her brother's house in Toronto. She loved the fresh air, the open spaces, and the greenery. During that time, she had looked for and found a small apartment not too far from Nimesh's place. Nimesh and Naomi helped her set it up, and then left her on her own. Maya got busy writing cover letters, updating her CV, and meeting people at schools and community colleges that Naomi had put her in touch with; Naomi was on the school board in Toronto. Nimesh was a cardiologist. Lisa was in her last year at high school, and busy with university applications.

Maya enrolled in a guidance counsellor's course at the University of Toronto. She worked hard, and made a few friends. They talked while in school, but it never went anywhere beyond that. She was older than many of her classmates who naturally didn't want to hang out with her. And the older ones had their own families to worry about after classes.

She saw Nimesh and Naomi only once every two to three weeks. They had their friends and Naomi's family who lived there. Maya felt lonely, especially on weekends. Sometimes she cooked Indian food for Nimesh and took it over to eat together with them, but after the first few times, they did not seem as welcoming. Nimesh told her that though he loved to have Indian food occasionally, he did not want it so often.

She stayed in touch with Rahul by email and Skype. She missed him intensely. She longed for Mumbai, and the warmth of the people back home. Rahul was happy to get her emails and calls, and said he missed her too.

After finishing the diploma, Maya started a part-time job as a counsellor at a high school, going in about twice a week. Soon, she got an email from Rahul to tell her that he was working on an art installation project with another artist hired by the city. The art was for the Victoria Terminus station area, and it was huge. He was excited about it, and just wanted to share the news with her. The money, too, was good. They were to complete the work in three months.

Maya was happy for him. She told him that she had just started working at the school, and that she now had some time to explore Toronto and its surroundings. She said that she would visit art galleries, and would let him know if she saw anything interesting.

After a while, her motivation to explore the city wore off. It was a fine city, but she felt alone. Once or twice she could interest a teacher from the school to accompany her to an art gallery, or a visit to an outlying park. Time was running out, and she had to decide if she wanted to live in Toronto, or return home.

Maya was invited to Lisa's graduation party, which was also a celebration of her admission to one of the best art schools in Canada. Maya remembered how much her niece had enjoyed *gajjar halva* on her visit to Mumbai, so she made a large quantity to take to the party. She dressed festively in Indian clothes, thinking that there would be a few other Indians as well.

Lisa opened the door when she arrived. After a moment's awkwardness, as Lisa took in her aunt's outfit from head to toe, she embraced her, and said, "Come on in. What do you have here?"

"I made you the carrot dessert you liked so much in Mumbai."

"Mom's in the kitchen. Why don't you give it to her; she will know where to put it." Then she ran off to her friends in the basement.

When she entered the kitchen, Nimesh said, "Maya, so glad you could come. Look Naomi, Maya's got us some *gajjar halva*."

Naomi looked up from the salad she was tossing, "Thanks, Maya. But we already have so much dessert. Let's put it in the fridge for now."

Nimesh guided her by the arm to the living room where the other guests were having drinks. Everyone stopped talking when they entered, some looking at her as if she had come from another planet. Nimesh suddenly became aware of what she was wearing, and looking a little embarrassed, he turned around and went to get her a drink. Maya broke the silence by talking to the people standing next to her, and slowly the chattering began again. But the rest of the guests left her alone.

After she had finished her drink, Maya mumbled an excuse and left the room. She looked out through a sliding door at the rain coming down. *What am I doing here?* she asked herself. *Nobody seems interested in getting to know me. How will I ever make friends in Toronto?*

Then she went into the kitchen. A couple of women were helping Naomi. Naomi exchanged glances with them, as they took food to the dining room. Maya felt excluded; she was not made to feel a part of the family at all. What was wrong with Naomi? She was unpredictable. She was so warm when she visited Mumbai, and welcoming when Maya had first arrived here. But now she was distant and cold. *Should I have a talk with her one of these days? Or should I talk to Nimesh?*

Her *gajjar halva*, which she had slogged over, was not out on the dessert table. When she asked Naomi, she said, "Not many people will like it here. They always find Indian desserts too sweet."

"I did not make it too sweet, and both Lisa and Nimesh like it."

"They can always have it later. Nimesh can take it for all his Indian colleagues at the hospital."

She hadn't enjoyed the evening. It had been tense for her, a strain. When she got home, she went to bed confused and tearful.

Her assignment with the school was now over, and she had been offered a job with a community college as a guidance counsellor. This was a full-time position, and Maya had two weeks to accept it. When she spoke with Rahul he said that if she liked it there, she should try it for a year.

"Do you really miss me?" she asked.

"Of course, I do. Mukul, Radhika, and I had dinner together last evening, and we were talking about you. Radhika is expecting a baby. I hadn't seen them in a while, because I've been working on the project till late in the evenings."

"How is your living arrangement working out?"

"It's fine. Chaya is often travelling during the week, so I have the apartment to myself."

"Well, I'll let you know if I accept the job or not," Maya said.

One evening, she asked Nimesh to come to her place so that she could talk to him. Naomi was busy with a school board event that night anyway. Maya told him what was on her mind: what she felt at the graduation party, how lonely she was, and that they were hardly spending any time together though they were close family. And she now had an important decision to make.

"Why is Naomi cold with me? She was different when you came to India."

"Naomi is a moody person, Maya. Also, when you came for the party you stuck out, with your Indian clothes and *gajjar halva.*"

"Well, I thought that there would be more of your Indian friends, and their wives who would be wearing Indian clothes. Lisa loves *gajjar halva*, and it was her party."

Nimesh said, "You have to understand Maya, that we've

had a life here now for twenty years. We cannot give all that up because you're here."

"No, of course not. I don't expect that. What I did expect was being sometimes included in your life, since I'm family. I'm grateful for all the help that you and Naomi gave me when I first arrived, but I thought that there would be more informal dropping by at each other's homes, and that we would spend more time together as a family."

Nimesh was quiet for a while. Then he said, "It's natural that you feel lonely here. You can never have the connections that you have in Mumbai, at this stage in your life, here. You will make some friends if you are working full-time. Both Naomi and I are busy with work as well as social events, so I don't know that we can spend much more time together. Maybe, I can drop by at your place occasionally, like I have today. Your decision to stay or not should not be based on that; you must really want to live here."

Since Maya did not respond right away, Nimesh put his arm around her. He said, "Do you really like this life here, and do you want to move to Canada?"

"I don't know. I should think more clearly." Maya had tears in her eyes.

Nimesh patted her back, and then he left. He had to pick up Naomi.

Rahul had been too busy with the project to talk on Skype, given the time difference. He replied cryptically to her messages, saying that he would write a long email when he had some breathing space.

She spent the next few days staying in most of the time, only stepping out for walks in the afternoons to clear her mind. She had only a week left to decide. Her thoughts strayed to Rahul frequently, not just as a friend, but as a significant other. His not having time for her at present, agitated her.

She decided to return to India. When Nimesh dropped by, she told him. He said, "I'm glad. Don't get me wrong. I'm glad because you don't look happy here. I think it is the right decision for you. You have a lot of people waiting for you back home."

Maya was relieved that the decision was made. Rahul was applying the last touches to the installation when she called him, so spoke briefly. He sounded pleased at the news of her return, and told her to send all her flight details so that he could come to the airport. She was disappointed that he was not ecstatic; but then he was preoccupied. He had not been engaged in such an important project before. Here was his chance to make it in the art world. He was glad that she would be back in Mumbai in time for the opening. It was to be a big affair.

Her last six weeks passed in blur. At the little farewell dinner party her brother hosted at their place a week before she was due to leave, Maya met people she had not met before. There were two Indian couples. Maya connected immediately with one of the wives who had grown up in Mumbai.

Then there was a new head of radiology from Nimesh's hospital. He was a Canadian in his late fifties. He had clear blue eyes, and straight blonde hair. His smile was open and warm. His wife had died of cancer five years ago. He wanted to know all about Maya, and about Mumbai, as he had never been to India. He said to Nimesh, "You kept your sister hidden for so many months. And now that I have met her, she is leaving." He took down Maya's email, and gave her his business card. His name was Mark Johnston. He said there was a chance he would be invited to a radiology conference in India next year, either in Mumbai or Delhi, and if he came, he would get in touch with her. Maya found him interesting, and she said that she looked forward to meeting him again. When he left the party, he shook hands with her, holding her hand a few seconds longer than usual.

Now that she was ready to leave, Maya couldn't get to Mumbai quickly enough. She boarded her flight, filled with anticipation. She had a whole month before college opened. Enough time to settle in, and see everyone again. She and Rahul could spend some time together. The opening of the installation was two weeks away. After that, he would be free.

Her flight landed at six in the evening and, as promised, Rahul was there to greet her. He grinned broadly when he saw her, and waved. As soon as she got to where he was waiting, he took the baggage cart from her and hugged her with an arm around her shoulders. As they headed out of the airport in her car, Rahul looked at his watch. "Oops," he said. "It is already seven-thirty. I must meet Nina ... the other artist, by nine. We have lots of work to do before the opening. Here, I've brought the invite for you. You can bring one friend, if you like."

"Oh, I thought you would have dinner with me."

"Sorry, but I'm going to be dreadfully busy until the opening. What do you think of the card?"

Maya looked at the card in her hand. "It's beautiful and very unusual. Did you design it?"

"No, Nina did."

They reached Maya's building and Rahul came up to help her with the luggage. They sat down for a few minutes, but Rahul was anxious to get going. "I have to leave. Nina and I have to finish up some things tonight."

"Why don't you have a quick bite and then go?" Maya said.

"I have to pick up some food for Nina anyway ... it will be a working dinner. You rest well. I will call you tomorrow."

Maya saw Rahul only once before the opening, at a cafe near Victoria Terminus. Just as they were finishing, Nina dropped by to grab a coffee. She was wearing jeans with a vibrant orange *kurta*. A leather bag was slung over her shoulder. Her thick hair was long and loose. Her dark brown eyes were her best feature. They were rimmed with kohl, and were vivacious and smiling. And when they looked at Rahul a new kind of light appeared in them. There was admiration in Rahul's eyes as he watched Nina talking. Maya thought Nina was probably in her mid-thirties, quite a bit younger than both of them.

"Rahul talks so much about you that I feel I already know you," Nina said,

"I hope he said all good things."

"Yes, of course. You must come for the opening next Friday," Nina smiled broadly.

"I wouldn't miss it. Both of you have worked so hard. Do I get a peek before that?"

Together they said, "No, you don't. You have to wait for the big day."

"The other night when Rahul cooked for me at his place," Nina said, "he made your favourite dish, *chole/puri*. He said it wasn't as good as yours. We'd been working so late, usually until midnight, that we needed a break." She looked at Rahul and smiled. Rahul returned the smile, the left corner of his mouth lifting just a little; the same smile that Maya had noticed at their first meeting so long ago.

Maya felt uncomfortable. She felt like an intruder, witnessing an intimate moment between a couple. She stood up and said, "You guys please go ahead and get to work. I will see you at the opening, and good luck." She felt a tight smile stretching her lips, as she bade them goodbye.

Sitting in the car in the evening traffic, she thought, *I'm being silly. They have been working together every day for almost six months. Naturally there is a professional connection. They have developed a relationship, part of which is also personal. It will evaporate once this project is done. I'm feeling like this because I haven't had any time with Rahul after coming back. We have a lot to catch up on.*

When Maya went to the opening, Rahul and Nina welcomed her, and Rahul showed her to her seat in the third row. The first two were for government officials and other VIPs. When the installation was unveiled, there was a sharp collective intake of breath from the audience, and then a thunderous round of applause. Rahul and Nina stood on either side of the installation, beaming at each other. It was an imposing piece of work, made with metal and wood, showing a modern metropolis, but with vestiges of a past glory in the background. There was an elaborate elephant drawn carriage with an umbrella, which Maya loved. The artists came centre stage, waved to the audience and hugged each other before making way for the minister's speech.

Rahul and Nina sat down together in the front row. There were several speeches, and a music and dance program. Mukul and Radhika sat next to Maya. While she and Radhika had a whispered conversation, Maya noticed Rahul's face close to Nina's ear; he was saying something to her, and then she turned to look at him and smiled warmly.

Maya left the exhibit without having had the opportunity to speak to Rahul or Nina; they had been surrounded by throngs of people the entire evening.

Rahul called the next evening. He said, "Where did you go? I was looking for you, then Mukul and Radhika said you had already left."

"I tried to talk to you before I left, but it was impossible."

"So, what did you think of the installation?"

"I loved it. It is a great piece of art. I especially like the elephant carriage. When can we meet properly, Rahul?"

"Soon, Maya. We need to tie up some loose ends before Nina leaves for Pune next week, to spend time with her parents."

Maya was preoccupied with lecture preparation, and faculty meetings before the new academic year began. Rahul called to say that he could have dinner with her after dropping Nina to the train station the next evening. Maya invited him home.

She came back early from the library, and changed into some new clothes that she had bought in Toronto. They were lounge pants with a flared bottom and a flowing tunic-like top. She applied eye make-up and lipstick, and instead of her usual diamond studs, wore turquoise dangling earrings to match her tunic. Perfume would be too much, she decided. After all, they were going to be at home.

When the doorbell rang, she ran to open the door, and when Rahul stepped in she enfolded him in an embrace, which he returned briefly. He said, "Hey, what's all this?"

"Just some clothes I bought in Toronto. Don't you like them?"

"Yes, but you look different. And make up for dinner at home?"

"Oh, I just felt like it. I've got some clothes for you too. See, there are two T-shirts."

Rahul opened the package. "What nice colours! Thank you."

After dinner, he kept looking at his phone. Maya said, "Are you late for something?"

"Oh no, just wondering why Nina hasn't messaged me yet; she must have reached Pune by now."

Rahul seemed restless. A little later, he said he was tired and should go to bed as the last few months had been brutal.

At the door, Maya asked what they should do the coming weekend. "A movie and dinner? I haven't seen a Bollywood movie in ages."

"Oh, I forgot to tell you. I'm going to Pune to meet some artists that Nina knows; there might be a project happening there soon."

Maya's face fell. "Call me when you have time," she said as evenly as she could muster.

When Rahul returned from Pune, he told Maya that talks about the project had started in earnest. "It's a lot of money," he said. "I can't let it go. I may even be able to rent my own apartment after this."

They did not meet as frequently as they used to before she went to Canada. And when they did meet, Maya felt that there was a distance, a new formality. Once Maya suggested a visit to an art exhibition, but Rahul had already seen it with Nina; though he did offer to accompany her if she wanted company. Maya did not see much point in discussing their current relationship, hoping that in time, they would be back on their old footing.

It was almost mid-term break when she received an email from Nimesh's friend, Mark. She hadn't thought about him since her return. After all, she had met him just once. He said that the conference was to be in Mumbai in mid-December. It would be over by the twentieth, and then he planned to travel around India for a couple of weeks, using Mumbai as his base. Could he contact her when in Mumbai? Did she have any suggestions for places to go to? She replied saying of course, he could. She suggested Delhi/Agra, Rajasthan, and Kerala as places he could visit.

A few weeks later, Mark's dates were fixed, and he said that he had decided to go to Rajasthan. Had she been there? Maya replied that Rajasthan was vibrant and colourful. Yes, she had been there, but fifteen or twenty years ago. It must have changed a lot since then, she told him.

Rahul's project in Pune was confirmed. He would be there from November to the end of February, at least. He would rent a studio. It was an installation art project near Ferguson College. He hoped that Maya would visit him there on some weekends, though he and Nina would be busy, working all week.

"Won't you come to Mumbai?" Maya said

"Yes, I will. But not more than once a month," he'd explained hurriedly. It seemed now, there was always someplace else he had to be.

What about us, Maya's heart cried out. *What place do I have in your life?* It was almost six months since she had returned from Toronto. Their relationship was different now, and she feared it would remain like that.

That night she woke up, breaking out in a sweat. When she got up to have a sip of water, she realized that she had dreamt again of the forest in the wall mural. Only this time, she had trembled with fright; she was alone, staring into the darkness.

* * *

It would soon be the second anniversary of her mother's death;

had she even grieved for her properly? Maya wondered. She had grieved for relationships with men that had ended, but then she had gone on to other relationships. With her mother, that was not possible. She was gone, and nobody else could take her place, ever. The first anniversary of her mother's death had gone by without arousing strong feelings in Maya. During her relationship with Rahul, her stint in Toronto, and then settling back into Mumbai life, time had flown. Though she did remember her mother at odd moments, she had not felt the deep bottomless vacuum she was experiencing now, after two years. Was it a delayed reaction?

After Rahul's temporary move to Pune, she saw her mother everywhere: in the kitchen, in the armchair, at the dining table. She remembered her warmth, generosity, and unassuming nature; her concern when Maya broke up with a man who had appeared promising. All things considered, her mother had been very liberal and modern in her outlook, even though she had been a conventional wife and mother.

Maya decided to write to Nimesh, reminding him of the anniversary. They had exchanged emails only once after her return to India. She told him that Mark had contacted her, and was coming to India. In his reply, Nimesh told her that Mark had laughingly said that maybe Maya could join him on the trip to Rajasthan. What did she think about that? Maya did not respond to that question, and it was soon out of her mind.

A month before he was due to arrive, Mark emailed her to give her his hotel details. He wrote that if he was not being too presumptuous, would she think of coming with him to Rajasthan? It would be holiday time for her too, wouldn't it? "Your brother knows me well," he said, "and I will take good care of you. And you would be a great guide for me, as I will be visiting India for the first time."

Maya had read the email late one evening, and she'd laughed it off; of course, he was joking, and of course she couldn't go. She would reply soon, she told herself.

She had put off replying to Mark for over a week. It was a Monday morning, and her driver was sick. She rushed to get dressed because she would have to take the bus to college. She looked out anxiously for the bus. The red double decker came thundering along, spewing exhaust, and the waiting mass of humanity inched forward. She climbed onto the bus, using her elbows to fight off men trying to push ahead of her. Lifting her cotton sari with one hand, Maya made her way to the top deck, finding a seat at the very front. As a young girl, she had always felt adventurous sitting on the top deck. The strong wind ballooned her sari out to the sides, and her hair blew into her face. Suddenly, a sense of excitement crept up her spine. *I'll go,* she said to herself, smiling. *I'll go to Rajasthan with Mark.* And she tucked her blowing hair behind her ears.

The Last Letter

❧

DEAREST BROTHER,
 I haven't written to you all for a long time, but time just slips through my fingers. In Mumbai, days and nights roll into one as I try and settle down with Anand. I have learned that he has quite a temper. I'm surprised because those few times we met before our marriage, he was quiet, and even somewhat detached when wedding details were discussed, but he did not seem short-tempered. So, often, appearances are deceptive.

It is difficult to get anything done in this city. You have to chase the phone man and the gas man until they make the connections for you, even after you give them a tip. And everything is expensive here. Anand and I sometimes argue about what is essential for our tiny flat and what is not.

I'm used to the open spaces in our village, and our house surrounded by green fields and trees. The only thing I can see from my tiny kitchen window is the next building, whose grimy peeling paint and garbage heap makes me want to vomit.

But don't think Mumbai is all ugly; for there are some very nice parts. We took the local train the other day. You won't believe how crowded our compartment was; I almost got pushed out the open door of the train! We went to see the Gateway of India and the Taj Mahal Hotel. What amazing structures! I stood there and couldn't move, my mouth open in wonder, until Anand pushed me along saying, "Don't stand there like a country bumpkin. Keep your wits about you, or someone will snatch your purse." On the way back, it was dark, so we got to see the Queen's Necklace—those are the lights of south Mumbai that glitter like diamonds. There are so many beautiful buildings from the English people, as well as many modern office buildings. It is my dream to live in south Mumbai, and Anand wants to live there as well. The far-flung northern suburb that we live in is very different, and oh, so remote from all this.

Anyway, enough about me. How are you? And Ma and Pa? Do give me all the news. I must cook the rice. Anand will be home soon.

Love to you all.

Surekha

* * *

Respected Pa and Ma,

Hope you are both in good health. I'm settling down well in Mumbai. We still need to buy more things for the house … utensils, some sheets, and curtains. I think everything will be done in a couple of months. The most important thing is that, finally, we have got a phone and gas connection, after having paid a bribe. I would be thrilled if you could come and visit me soon. I'm sitting on our new couch and writing to you. The fabric is soft like velvet. The colour is a deep red, like your bindi, Ma.

I cook what we eat at home, but Anand prefers Mumbai food, like *pau bhaji, chole, biryani*. He says that he will buy me a cookbook. I can't imagine cooking from a book. That would be strange. I would rather ask someone, but who can I ask? I don't know anyone yet.

I long for the fresh air of Nagda. Here, because of the many cars and buses, the air stinks of petrol fumes. I must get used to it. Mumbai is an exciting city. There are so many people, and so many things happening. I hear on TV about dance programs, music concerts, book festivals, sari sales, TV and phone launches, new restaurants, and coffee shops. The list is endless. The city pulses with an energy that creeps into your blood, and you too want to be doing something all the time. Everyone is rushing from one place to the next. No one has time to stop and talk to you. One morning, when I was at the egg stall, I asked a lady where she bought her purse because it was big, and the colour was like that of wet mud. I wanted to touch it, but she moved away from the stall so quickly, that she almost dropped the eggs she had just bought. While I stood there waiting my turn, she put her dark glasses on her head, glared at me, and walked away, without even saying *namaste*.

Do you miss me? Please ask Brother to write for you and give me all the news.

Your daughter,
Surekha

* * *

My Dear Brother,

It's been almost two months since I last wrote. The monsoons are here in full swing, and the city is a mess. I keep thinking of the peacocks dancing outside our house, and the high wheat grass swaying in the wind. Are we going to have a good crop this year? It is a good monsoon. At least, that's what they are saying on TV. I have the TV on as I write to you, and in the news, they said that there will be another heavy rainfall tomorrow.

We have a fully running house now, and I wish you could come to Mumbai to visit. I'm lonely. I haven't made any friends. If I talk to people in the hallways, Anand doesn't like it. He says I must be careful of people in this big bad city — you never know what designs they have on you, and especially the men. That nice uncle, Mehtaji, is so friendly. But I dare not look up to meet his eyes if Anand is with me. He dug his fingers hard into my arm the last time I smiled at the old man.... Oops, I did not mean to tell you. Please forget it, and don't worry. I can take care of myself. Don't read this out to

Ma and Pa, please! I'm sure you first skim through my letter before reading it out loud.

How are Kamala and Minu? Tell them I value their friendship more than ever now.

Hope you're not working too hard in the rains.

I should get up and close the window. The wind is blowing hard, and it will bring in all the dust. It will soon start raining again, and my new yellow curtains will get wet and dirty.

Love,
Surekha

* * *

My Dear Kamala,

How are you? You should come and see our flat. It is tiny, but I have filled it with bright colours. People here call it "cozy." You will like Mumbai, I'm sure, because there is constant activity, and I know you like to be doing something all the time. Who knows? You might even catch a glimpse of your favourite film star, Sharukh Khan.

Brother told me that your parents are looking out for a boy for you. How do you feel about that? I hope they find someone who lives in Mumbai; then we can perhaps live in the same building.

The girls here dress like movie actresses. I hardly see them in saris or *ghaghara*, or even in Punjabi dresses. Most of them wear tight jeans and a blouse, or a short *kurta*. There is no *dupatta* to cover their breasts. Some wear very short dresses, and the straps on the dress look like bra straps. I feel so embarrassed when I see them. But I do want to buy jeans when we have some extra money. Right now, we have spent everything on setting up the house. I look very old-fashioned compared to these Mumbai girls.

You must come here right after your marriage is fixed. Otherwise you won't have time for quite a while. I will show you all the sights, and you can taste *bhel puri* and *pau bhaji*.

Let me know as soon as everything is decided. I pray to God that you find a good match.

Good luck.

Surekha

* * *

Dearest Brother,

Is everything fine? You have not replied to my last letter. Did you get it, or did it get lost in the mail?

Did the water seep into our house this year? There must be lots of little waterfalls and streams outside. Remember how we sailed paper boats in the streams? How fast they used to go! And we would run along and jump into the streams to catch them before they disappeared. I felt happy then, and oh, so free.

Mumbai is depressing in the rains. I haven't seen the sun for days. There are hardly any trees or flowers to break the monotony of grey cement buildings and the grey skies. Our building is new, and yet there is already a leak in our bedroom ceiling. I must place a bucket under it. The dripping drives me crazy all day. Anand says he doesn't feel like coming home, it's so annoying, and that I should do something about it. But what can I do? I have already complained to the building manager several times.

I was sick the last few days. I had what the doctor called "gastroenteritis." I think, that's how they call it. That is diarrhea and vomiting. I think it was because I ate *bhel puri* from the hawker who comes to the building every evening. I was so bored, and I had to get out of the apartment. I didn't tell Anand that; he would be mad. He had warned me not to eat hawker food in the monsoons. Going to the doctor is expensive. But I'm fine now.

I think and dream a lot when there is nothing to do, especially in the evenings. I dream that I'm loved deeply by my husband; I dream of having lots of children, a nice house, and many friends. And, of course, I dream of spending a lot of time with all of you even though I'm now married. I know that Anand dreams of making pots of money in Mumbai. What else does he want from life? I don't know.

Brother, what are your dreams these days? I'm sure you are waiting for the right girl to come along, so you can get married and start a family, and that you hope for a good crop to make all that possible. I pray that everything you wish for comes true. I sit on the couch waiting for my husband to return. I stare at the walls as I think about how to put my feelings into words and then onto this paper. It's not easy to say exactly what I think and feel. I'll turn off the TV now. I keep it on most of the evening for company. But how much TV can I watch? It's giving me a headache. It is late. Anand is still not home, but I will warm up the food.

Please write soon.

Love,

Surekha

* * *

My dear Brother,

I'm sitting here at our little dining table to write to you, so that I can check on the *dal* that is cooking in the kitchen. It is so hot. The window is open, but there is no breeze. I can feel sweat running down my back, though I've knotted up my hair into a bun, and am wearing a thin cotton *kurta*. The building children, who were playing downstairs earlier in the evening, have gone home, and the sound of traffic is fading, as people are back with their families; except my husband.

The monsoons are almost over, and the traffic is much better, but Anand is always late. He never comes home before midnight. He grumbles about the office, and about the amount of work he has to do. He says he is working overtime to pay for everything we have bought for the house.

I have made a few friends in the building, but Anand doesn't know yet. We visit one another, and I tell them about quilt-making. I tell them about our fields, and all the work that needs to be done from morning till night. They teach me how to cook new dishes. I enjoy being with these women. They tell me about Mumbai — about the buildings where the rich live, about Mumbai's famous dance bars, Chowpatty beach, the Dharavi slum, and other things.

Last Sunday Anand took me to Juhu beach to eat *pani puri*. The small crisp *puri* is filled with tamarind-mint water, and when you pop it whole into your mouth, there is a burst of tangy, spicy, and sweet flavours combined with the crunch of the *puri*.

How is Pa? Hope he does not get fever this year. Ma must be working so hard without me there to help her.

I want to get a job. I'm scared to talk to Anand about it. Brother, what do you think of my earning money? I don't know what kind of work I would find, and how and where. Maybe I can teach quilt-making at the women's centre. It's close by. I'll have to pick up courage to go in and find out.

It's eleven pm. I'm not sure what Anand does in the office so late every night. He doesn't like me questioning him. I tell him that I see other men returning home in time for dinner. He just grunts and tells me to mind my own business. It's so dreary to be alone all evening, and not have anyone to talk to. I'll have my dinner now, once again, alone. At home, we all sat down together in the kitchen while Ma made us hot *roti*. You and Pa would finish eating and get back to work. I sat with Ma while she ate, and we talked about so many things.

Love,
Surekha

* * *

Dear Ma and Pa,

You're going to be very proud of me. I teach quilt-making and earn two hundred rupees per hour. I had my first class today. There were ten students in the room. Thanks to you, Ma, I love quilting and am quite good at it, at least compared to these city women. I'm excited to be able to go out and meet some other people. And yes, I have permission from my husband. I should put the money in the bank and earn interest, he says, instead of frittering it away. He will need to teach me about all that.

How is Dadi? Is her knee better? I hope she can walk by herself now. I'm sure you miss my help with her, and with all the housework.

You told me before I got married that I should obey my husband and I'm trying to do that. I want him to be happy with me. I only wish he would talk with me a little more and come home earlier. Then we could have dinner together, go for a short walk, and watch some TV shows before going to sleep. Maybe he is worried about his job, and about how I am taking to life in Mumbai; and about being responsible for me, and then later, for a family.

I wore the red and gold sari you gave me for my first day of class. I should change now, so that it doesn't get oil and turmeric stains on it when I start cooking. I'm going to make *aloo-gobi* and *dal*. The cauliflower doesn't taste anything like the ones from our fields. I try to make it tastier by adding more spices. Will think of all of you while I eat. Don't know when Anand is coming home.

Love,
Surekha

* * *

Dearest Brother,

Now I teach quilt-making twice a week and I love it. We gossip, laugh, and sing as we work. The women's centre is a ten-minute walk, and it's so good to get out of this apartment. Anand doesn't seem to be too concerned. I bring in a little bit of money. Anyway, he is in his own world these days. He smiles, laughs, and whistles. Almost like a teenager.

He comes home so late, that sometimes he does not even eat

dinner. He has bought a cell phone. That is not an unnecessary expense according to him, and he is busy learning how to use it. He says I can call him anytime.

Tomorrow is Mumbai Bandh. Everyone is talking about it. Nothing will be open. We won't even get milk. All offices and schools are closed. Anand will have a holiday, though he isn't too happy about it, God knows why. He says that the Opposition Party wants to show that it can bring Mumbai to a grinding halt.

How is Dadi doing? I do miss her *ladoo*. I bought some at the sweet shop down the road, but my grandma's are the best in the whole world. These were dry. They're stingy with the ghee here, and I thought Mumbai was a rich city. Nobody even feeds the dogs properly. They find something to eat in the garbage, just imagine. No *roti* soaked in warm milk for them. I remember how we used to feed Sita before she died. Her puppies must be big now. Did you give a few away?

I wish I could come home for Diwali, but Anand says we can't waste money. The markets are crowded these days because everyone is shopping for the festival. I look at the beautiful saris and the gold jewellery in the shops when I walk to my classes. I sometimes go in and feel the soft silk, and try a gold choker around my neck. I wonder if Anand will buy me something for our first Diwali together, but I dare not ask.

Enjoy all the goodies that Dadi and Ma make, and you can eat my share as well!

Lots of love to everyone for the festival.

Surekha

* * *

Dearest Kamala,

Congratulations! I am so happy to know that you're engaged to Raju. I remember him as a shy, quiet young man, cycling down the market road in our village. I think that he and Anand were together for a while in the village school. Then Anand went to Mumbai to take the business course. I hope you will be very happy together.

Kamala, I'm sitting here on my bed after lunch, thinking of how to tell you. I just washed the tears off my face and made up my mind to write to you. I don't want to dampen your enthusiasm, but I don't want you to be disillusioned and miserable. So, I'm going to tell you a few things that I have experienced, and I pray fervently that your experience is very different. Anand does not seem interested in getting to know me at all. He comes home late and goes right to sleep. He usually does not even have dinner with me.

Maybe once a week, or even once in two weeks, he does "his business" on me, without caring what I feel. It could be anyone under him. There is no affection, no romance. Sometimes, I feel he is thinking of another woman. Please don't breathe a word of this to anyone. I know you won't. I had to tell someone. I have written to Brother that he comes home at midnight, but not that I suspect he has another woman. If he cares for another woman, why did he not marry her?

Anyway, I'm not sure, but I spend hours thinking about this. The tears come very easily to my eyes, and then I so desperately want to be with you. I rage at God. Why did I get such a man? How were my parents to know? He comes from a good family, is well educated, and has a job in Mumbai ... what a good match!

Every day we talk only about meals and how much cash I need to run the house. I try to talk to him about how I feel about things in Mumbai, about something I saw on TV, but he does not respond. I'm not sure if he even listens. He did take me out a couple of times to see Mumbai soon after our marriage, but we have not gone out together since then.

There, I feel better after having told you the truth about my marriage. At least, that is the truth right now. Maybe, Anand just needs time to get used to me and to being married. Your marriage I am sure will be happier. The little that I know of Raju makes me certain he will indeed make a wonderful husband.

Now, for the the good part. Brother must have told you that I'm teaching quilt-making to a group of women at a women's centre. I've also made some friends. A man in the office there looks after the accounts. He is such a gentleman. He treats me with respect and always asks how I'm settling down in Mumbai. His name is Suresh Kakkar.

This will be your last Diwali at home. Next year will be different, in your in-laws' house. Good wishes for the festival. Let me know when your wedding date is fixed. I will try to come.

Lots of love,
Surekha

* * *

Dearest Brother,

There was no love or joy for me this Diwali.

From our window, we could see the firecrackers. Most of them make loud noises, and everyone here likes those more than the pretty *phuljhari* we burst in the village. I made *halva-puri*. Anand and I went to the temple, but he would have rather stayed at home. He was grumpy most of the time. Tell Ma that I made a colourful *rangoli* design outside our door, and lit a few oil lamps. Everyone from the building loved my *rangoli,* but Anand didn't say anything about it at all.

He is obsessed with his new phone. He says that he is learning to use it. He goes out to the hallway of our floor often, and I hear him laughing and talking. But he hardly ever laughs with me. Make sure you only read the selected bits of my letters to Ma and Pa.

Now, some exciting news. My quilt- making students have made enough quilts for us to have a small exhibition in December. We're all working very hard. I work on my quilt till late at night, when Anand returns. I have done a few patches so far — our house with trees, dancing peacocks, and you and

Pa working in the fields. I will now make patches from my life in Mumbai. What shall I make? Buses and cars? Beggars eating from garbage dumps? Shops? Maybe I should make something nice, like the Queen's Necklace I told you about, or the vast ocean, though they are not part of my life here. I will let Ma know how it comes along. I showed it to Anand, but he barely glanced at it. He doesn't talk to me too much, except for asking for another *roti* or a fresh towel. I told him about the exhibition, and that Suresh sahib, in the women's centre, wants me to take more classes. Anand seemed miffed at the attention I'm getting. I feel he might be a little jealous. But I'm sure all of you are happy for me.

If anyone takes photographs of the quilts, I will mail them to you, and then you can see what my students have done. As for my quilt, I will bring it home when I come, so that whenever you use it, you will think of me. I must finish the patch I'm working on before going to bed. I sit on the floor with my back against the sofa, the quilt spread out in front of me. I need to push the small centre table to the side. There is so little space here. At home, Ma and I used to sit on the string bed, under the shade of the huge banyan tree, and when I got tired of working on the quilt, I would get up and swing from the branches hanging low.

Love,
Surekha

* * *

Brother,

I'm confused. Last week when I called Anand on his cellphone to ask him to buy bread because I thought he would be walking home from the station, I heard a woman talking to him, and laughing. I asked him who it was. He said, "I don't know what you're talking about. It must be someone walking behind me." And when he finally got home, he could not look at me. He slept outside on the sofa.

Yesterday, I was scared. It was two am, and he wasn't home. I heard sounds outside the main door, as if someone was trying to open it. When I went out to the hall from my bedroom, the sounds suddenly stopped. With trembling hands, I dialled Anand's number. He sounded strange when he finally picked up the phone. Was he sleeping? When I told him what had happened, he just laughed, and said nobody would try to enter our apartment, as there was nothing valuable to steal. Then I heard a rustling — maybe of clothes or sheets — and he abruptly hung up. He came home an hour later and just went to bed. I think he is sleeping with another woman, but I can't be sure.

Don't read any of this to Ma and Pa.

Surekha

***

My Dear Brother,

Our exhibition was a great success. Suresh Kakkar sahib commended the work we had done. So many people from the buildings close by came, and of the twenty-five quilts that we had displayed, nineteen were sold. I'll send the photographs soon. There's even one of me receiving flowers from my students! There was small mention of the exhibition in the community newspaper. As more women have enrolled in the class, Kakkar sahib said that they would give me three hundred rupees per hour instead of the two hundred that they have been paying me. I will save the money and send some of it to you. With the rest, I will buy myself a new sari, or jeans, as that's what everyone in Mumbai wears.

Kamala's wedding will take place in May, you write. She is so lucky that she will live in the village even after her marriage. If I save enough money, I can come for her wedding. I'm excited just thinking about it.

You say that you have not mentioned my problems at home, and that I should just do what Anand says. Brother, believe me, I'm trying to be a good wife, and will wait and hope that things change. Let's just keep it between us for now. You sound worried, and I'm sorry, but I had to tell you. Sometimes, I just want to do something bad to him, like shout and scream, hit and punch, or even draw blood by scratching him hard with my nails. No, you know I'm not going to do that.

Is it very cold in the village? Mumbai is always hot, especially in the afternoons. Sankranti will be here in two weeks, and I will miss all the fun of the kite festival at home. How big is the kite that you're going to fly? Hope your kite is the king of the skies, and destroys all others.

I will make *tilpapdi* and take it to my friends in the building, and some for my students. Even sesame seeds and *jaggery* are expensive here. It is my friends and students who keep me going.

With good wishes for Sankranti.

Love,

Surekha

* * *

My Dear Kamala,

Only four months left for your wedding! Preparations must have already started. You should come to Mumbai for the shopping, but of course, it will cost much more. But it would give you an excuse to come and stay with me for a few days. Have you checked out the stores in Rangpur? I went to the new shop near the station for my shopping. It has so much more variety than our village.

My quilt exhibition went well, and more women want to take my classes. I'll be getting more money per hour from now on.

You and Brother have been talking about Anand and me, I know. I have written to him about my suspicions, and he must have told you the details. I did something very naughty last week —I made a big tear in one of Anand's favourite shirts. It must be his woman's favourite, since he wears it every

Saturday evening. But he didn't notice it when he went out. He was fuming when he returned home late at night, but I pretended to be asleep, and couldn't stop laughing under the covers. Next Saturday, I should put some sleeping tablets in his tea so that he falls asleep and doesn't go out. What will his mistress say then? I wouldn't dare to do that. What if I put too many tablets by mistake and something happens to him? I would go to jail. I was always full of pranks in school. Do you remember how we poured water on the teacher's seat, just before Mr. Singh's class?

I have mentioned Suresh to you, haven't I? I meet him every time I go to class. I think he looks out for me on Tuesdays and Thursdays, and makes it a point to come out of his office to greet me. He even offered me tea and biscuits once after class. Kamala, I think he likes me, and I like him too. I wish he wouldn't come out of his office to see me, because I feel shy and uncomfortable, and I'm sure he notices that I get red in the face. But I do love to see him. I don't know what to do about my feelings, or about the way he looks at me. Kamala, do you feel that way when you see Raju? You and your parents must be meeting him and his family often to discuss the wedding details. Does he look at you in a special way?

Write to me and tell me everything, absolutely everything, about the wedding preparations. It would be such fun if we were together. Nagda is so far away. It would take at least a day and a half for me to get there.

Love,
Surekha

* * *

My Dear Brother,

What can I say? Anand has asked me to stop teaching at the centre. Let me tell you what happened. He came home at five pm last evening, and I was not yet home from my class. When I opened the door about an hour later, I was surprised and started to say, "Why are you...?"

Before I could complete the question, he said, "Why? Why? This is my home, that's why! And why were you not at home?"

I said, "I just finished the quilting class. I'm asking only because you never come home until midnight. What happened? She doesn't want to meet you anymore?"

He was so angry. He said, "Shut your mouth! I'm the one who asks questions, not you. I have a high fever and my throat is hurting. Make me ginger tea."

I brought him the tea and sat down. Sipping the tea, he said, "I want you to stop teaching. I don't need the few thousand rupees you make each month ... a pittance. You think you are great, having exhibitions, getting your name in the local paper. But you can't look after your husband. You are not here to serve me when I come home sick."

With that, he drained his cup and went to bed.

I continued to sit, trembling all over. *He is not going to stop me from doing what I love,* I said to myself. My eyes were stinging with unshed tears, but after a few moments I calmed down. I resolved to have it out with him after he has recovered.

He says that he earns enough, and that he doesn't need the measly sum I get at the end of every month. I think he is just plain jealous of the little enjoyment I have, of my friendships, and of the recognition I get in the community around here.

If I don't have my quilt-making class, I have nothing to do, nothing to look forward to. I will die of boredom and loneliness, Brother.

I know that once you advised me to do everything that my husband asked me to do, but I cannot do that anymore. I will not give up so easily. Mumbai has made me tough.

I will take care of myself. Try not to worry too much.
Surekha.

* * *

Dearest Brother,

I was glad to receive your letter, with Ma and Pa's words as well. I miss all of you so much.

Ma is asking about a grandchild, since I've been married for over a year now. After another year, perhaps. After we're more comfortable with one another. Anand comes home late, and on Sundays he sleeps most of the day. I don't even know if he wants a child with me.

Anyway, about the classes —I won! I fought and screamed and cried, and asked him to give me one good reason why I should stop. He finally walked out of the house yelling, "Do what you want!" and slammed the door shut. So, I went back to class. I had missed a couple of weeks, but Suresh sahib said that they would still pay me for the eight hours I missed, because on several occasions I have been there longer.

Anand doesn't take me anywhere. Most Saturday evenings he goes off on his own, all dressed up and smelling of cologne. I'm sure he goes to see the woman I've heard when I have called him. When I ask him about it, he doesn't answer. At times, I feel like tearing my hair out and just walking out. Why am I here with him? He doesn't care for me, doesn't talk to me, and doesn't want to go out with me. Why did he marry me?

You may see me at our doorstep in the village soon. I will beg, borrow, or even steal the money for the train fare and come home.

Surekha

*   *   *

Brother,

I'm sorry that you had to spend money on the DO NOT LEAVE telegram. I know, I know. Leaving will only create more problems. I wrote that in utter frustration. But I feel that way more and more with each passing day, since there is no change in Anand.

Do Ma and Pa know now? Do you think they could talk to his parents in the next village? But what will that do? They will only say that something is wrong with me, and that I'm not able to adjust to Mumbai. And even if I did come home, they would know, and then I'd have to go and live with them. They would treat me even worse than Anand does.

My thoughts turn towards Kamala, and her impending marriage often. Tell her that.

Love,
Surekha

* * *

Respected Ma,

How are you? I wish you were with me now.

Ma, I long to eat the *ladoo* that you and Dadi make. Can you tell me how to make them? Brother can write the recipe down as you speak. I hope it is not too difficult, because you see, I do tire easily these days. In fact, I'm sitting in bed, resting against the pillows, as I write to you. Ma, you're going to have a grandchild soon after Diwali. I hope this makes you happy. I'm happy because I'll have someone to love and care for. And if there is enough money, I can come home to have the baby.

Don't worry Ma, and tell Pa not to worry as well. It's not good for his heart. Asha, the lady who lives downstairs has two children — one ten-year-old boy and a seven-year-old girl. And she is giving me a lot of advice. She also brings me some food when she can.

Did you feel nauseous when you were carrying us? I feel sick every morning, but it gets better as the day progresses. I want to be with you, but Anand is taking good care of me, and sends his regards.

Your loving daughter,
Surekha.

* * *

Dearest Brother,

How do you feel about being an uncle? I'm sure you're wondering how I feel, given the situation with Anand. To be honest, I feel numb most of the time. The rare twinge of excitement soon disappears with the nausea and vomiting, and then I'm left drained and depressed. When I told Anand that I was with child, his eyes lit up briefly, but that was it. His behaviour has not changed, and he continues to stay out late.

I'm so lucky to be friends with Suresh sahib at the women's centre. He is a little older than Anand, but he is soft-spoken and gentle. This is the second time that he has invited me for tea to his office, and I enjoy talking to him. He has another job, but helps a few times a week with administration and accounts, as a volunteer.

On Tuesday, after I came out of the classroom, I saw him talking to the janitor. When he saw me, he said, "How are you, Surekhaji?" He said that I looked tired. "Come to my office. We can have a cup of tea, and you can rest before you walk home." That was so considerate of him. He realizes that I'm expecting, as I'm showing now. He asked me about all of you in the village. He said, "It must be difficult for you to get used to a new life in the city. You must miss your family. Your husband must be taking good care of you in your situation." I blushed and looked down. I could not answer. When I looked up at him, he saw my wet eyes. He looked concerned, and offered me another biscuit. I left soon after that. He walked me to the entrance of the centre, and patted me on the back. He said, "We will meet next week. Take good care of yourself."

Do you think you can come and see your nephew or niece soon after Diwali? I'm so sad that there will be no one from my family when my first child is born.

P. S. I'm enclosing the pictures from my exhibition. Show them to Ma and Pa. Don't read them the letter.

Surekha

* * *

Respected Ma and Pa,

Greetings. I made the *ladoo!* And they are good, but not as good as Dadi's. I'm trying to follow as many of the instructions you have given me about rest and diet as I can. Both you and Pa say I should listen to devotional music and have pure thoughts, as these will benefit the baby. Also, you say that the most important thing is to be happy and cheerful. I'm happy, except when I miss you.

There is a water shortage in Mumbai, and it is getting hotter every day. We get water for two hours in the morning and one hour in the evening. There will be mangoes on our trees in about a month's time. I have started a new quilt with three of my students, and on my patch, I'm making our mango grove. The trees will be laden with the golden fruit. Mangoes are very expensive here. I don't think I can even afford to have one mango a day, let alone the five or six I used to suck on at home.

The nausea and vomiting are better, and I'm well. I only wish you could be with me, Ma, when the baby is born. I'm scared. But I don't think I will be able to come home for the delivery. Anand says he doesn't want to spend the money, since we are just managing to make ends meet.

Pa, I hope you're well and not exerting yourself too much in the fields. Who is massaging your feet every evening now? I used to grumble when you asked me to do that, but now I miss our conversations. They were so special, with just you and me.

Your loving daughter,
Surekha.

* * *

Dearest Brother,

You're right. There is no need to get Ma and Pa anxious, and to tell my in-laws. If Anand knows that I've told you, things will only become worse. He used to drink whisky once or twice a week when we were first married, but now he drinks regularly, and much more. His speech is not normal when he comes home, and he sometimes staggers through the door. But for the child's sake, I should keep quiet.

Soon, I will start preparing for the baby. I will get a cot from Asha, but I will need to buy other things. I will do it in the last two months. Right now, I just want to keep well, and be as happy as possible. I try not to think of what the child will come to know about his or her father. He or she will sense my sadness very early on, but I will try to cover it up as much as possible. I will wait to hear it say "Ma," for it to take its first step. I imagine running around with my child, playing hide and seek, laughing and singing with it. The joy of watching my baby grow up will wash away all unhappiness; it is his or her future that I will look forward to.

The only people I can talk to are Asha and Suresh. Suresh makes me smile. But tongues will wag if I go to his office often. He is single. I hope he finds a good wife. He will make a wonderful husband and father.

I worry that if Anand gets drunk often, he will not be able to work, and he will be ill. Who will pay the rent? What will happen to the child then? For now, I live only for the birth of the baby.

Love,
Surekha

* * *

Dear Kamala,

You will be a married woman in less than a month. Is everything ready? You must be excited, and a little nervous. How is Raju? I'm sure he knows he's very lucky to get someone as sweet and beautiful as you.

By now you must know about the worsening situation between me and Anand. Also, about Anand's drinking. Anyway, I don't want to burden you with this just before your wedding. You also know the happy news that I'm going to be a mother. You must come and see your best friend's baby. Kamala, it is wonderful to have a life growing inside you, a life you're solely responsible for, a life to protect, love, and cherish forever.

I wish I could be there for your big day, just as you were there for mine. Enjoy the celebration. Don't think that all men are like my husband — unfaithful, uncaring, and completely self-absorbed. Your Raju, I'm sure, is a decent man. Have faith. Your goodness will enable you to overcome the initial difficulties all marriages go through. You will have a lot of help and support, as you will be amongst family and friends. Not like me, far away from anything familiar, tucked away in an apartment in Mumbai, where no one knows or cares about what's going on behind closed doors.

When is the pre-wedding music party? Have you decided on the henna design for your hands? How many sweets did all the aunties make for the guests? Oh, my mouth is watering. Here no one uses ghee; they use something called Dalda, which not real ghee.

How many brothers and sisters does Raju have? How old are they? I'm sure you will have lots of company. It's so lonely here with no one in the house. Everyone's doors are locked. You can't just go in and out of your neighbour's house. You must call them up first, and ask if they have time to see you and talk to you. Just imagine. I'm getting used to it. That's just the way it is here.

Do write to me after the wedding, when you have time. Good luck. Be happy, and above all, trust in God.

Lots of love and a big hug,
Surekha

* * *

Dearest Brother,

I got your letter this evening. You say Pa is coughing a lot, and has become very thin. How is he now? Have you taken him to our traditional doctor? If that doesn't work, take him to the English doctor in the town. I'm enclosing all the money I have saved from my teaching.

You said that Ma was anxious because I had not written for a long time. Break the news gently to her. Brother, I have lost my baby. It happened last month, and I was too weak to write. Read what I write next carefully, and only tell Ma what you think she should know, leaving out the bits about Anand and Suresh. I'm too tired to write two letters.

It was Saturday evening, and Anand was getting ready to go out. I started feeling dizzy, and I told him that it would be better if he stayed home with me. He said I would feel better if I rested quietly, and that he would come back soon. So, I rested. The last thing I remember was getting up to go to the bathroom, and then I must have blacked out. When I woke up again, maybe about an hour later, I was on the bathroom floor. There was blood on the floor and my clothes were wet. I somehow managed to get up and called Anand, but he did not pick up. At that moment, I thought I was going to die. But I said to myself, *no, I can't die like this*. I almost blacked out again, but I forced myself to be alert and dial my friend Asha's number. She came running, but her husband was travelling, and we needed a man, so I told her to call Suresh. They took me to the hospital by taxi.

They said it was a miscarriage, and that they had brought me to hospital in the nick of time.

Suresh sat with me. Asha had to return home to her children. She waited up for Anand to come home, and told him what had happened. When Anand came to the hospital that night, he couldn't even walk straight, and his speech was slurred. He jabbed his finger into Suresh's chest, and told him rudely to go, because he could take care of his wife. Suresh was reluctant to leave, but I nodded to him, and he left, looking at Anand with disgust. After that, the only words Anand said to me were, "You could not even give me a son. You lost him." Then he sat down in the chair Suresh had just vacated, and promptly fell asleep. I was at the hospital for two days.

Asha comes to be with me whenever she can. She is a comforting presence. She tells me that I can always have another child. I don't know if I want another. With a womanizing, drunk father, what future will the child have?

I'm getting my strength back slowly, but I don't feel like eating much. Tell Ma that the doctor said that I'll be okay in a few weeks. Anand still doesn't return home before midnight.

Please take Pa to the English doctor.

Surekha.

***

My Dear Brother,

It was a great comfort to read Ma's words that you wrote for her. Faith is everything, she says. Yes, she's right. Faith in God and in myself has kept me going these last two years of marriage. Teaching quilt-making has helped and I have met people who helped me rise above the problems in my life. Ma is referring only to my miscarriage, of course.

But Brother, now my faith in my own strength, and my trust in God are wavering. I was so looking forward to the baby. It would have been the centre of my life and it would have given my life meaning. Why did God take even that away from me? What did I do to deserve such a tragedy? I know there are no answers to these questions. We have always been taught that God knows best. God must have had a reason to take away my child. Maybe, I was not capable of looking after it, or perhaps, Anand will lose his job because he might go to work drunk. What would happen to the child then? But I feel a great emptiness in my heart and in my womb, a hollowness that nothing can fill.

Now, can you believe this? Anand is accusing Suresh of taking advantage of me, and so, even though I'm strong enough, he does not want me to go to the centre to teach. Suresh is the perfect gentleman, and I will go and see him soon. I will ask for his advice. Maybe I can go and teach without Anand knowing about it. Anyway, what right does he have to tell me what to do? I will do whatever I like!

But, I'm also afraid. If he finds out, he could get violent and beat me. So far, he has not raised his hand against me, only his voice. But when people are drunk, they are like animals. I think of Gagan in our village. He would get drunk on the local country liquor, miss work even during harvest time, and when his wife did not give him food because there was no money, he would beat her. He died soon after I left, didn't he?

My heart goes out to my dead child. It cries out. I suddenly see the baby on my bed, smiling at me. I stretch out my arms to pick it up, but embrace only air. Then I'm jolted back to reality. There is nothing — only my tears falling on the sheets like rain.

Please pray for me, Brother.

Yours,

Surekha

* * *

My Dearest Friend Kamala,

How are you? I heard that the wedding went well, and that you were the radiant bride. But how do you feel? Do you feel afraid of your in-laws? Are you happy when you're with Raju? He must be a loving husband. How was your wedding night? You can tell me all about it. No one else is going to read your letter. It will be a while before you feel that his house is your home. But since you're so close to your parents' house, you can visit them often. Do send me some photographs of the wedding, when you can.

You must have heard that I had a miscarriage. Everyone says I can try again after a few months. But I'm not sure. Should I have a child at all? With the kind of husband I have, it would be comforting to at least have a child to love, but what will it think of its father? Will Anand be able to support a child? Anand and I rarely sleep together. He returns home from his mistress spent, and falls asleep, without talking to me, or even looking at me. Kamala, I don't know what to do. In your letter before your wedding you said I should leave him, or even divorce him, but where will the money for a lawyer come from? Has anyone in our village ever been divorced? You must be reading a lot of modern novels to suggest that. What will Ma and Pa say? What will the whole village say if I go back to my parents? You know, Brother tells me to wait it out and see what happens. He has not told anyone at home. It is a good thing Ma and Pa can't read.

I see the child that would have been, running away from me and hiding under the bed. I see it sleeping in my lap as I sing a lullaby. I see myself feeding it *halva*. These visions just deepen my melancholy. The centre of my life is gone even before it could come into this world.

I'll tell you a little secret. My feelings for Suresh are becoming stronger. Are you shocked that a married woman can say such a thing? But what can I do? My husband does not care for me. If he did, I would surely love him, and not look at another man. I think of him when I'm home alone in the evenings. Suresh takes a genuine interest in me. Brother knows that Suresh and I are friends, but not about my feelings for him. There is nothing to be done about it. Suresh is too good a person to get into a relationship with a married woman, even though he knows the truth about my husband. And I? I'm tempted, but would feel ashamed, and wouldn't dare to approach him — I am still Anand's wife.

After you and Raju settle down, you should both come for a visit. Who knows, Anand may change a little when he sees how Raju treats you.

Stay well and be happy.

Your best friend,

Surekha

* * *

Dearest Brother,

I realize from your last letter that you are very stressed. You are worried about Pa, about me, and about money. I'm not even teaching, otherwise I would send you all the money I earned. Try not to worry about me. There is nothing to be done right now. You told me not to go to the centre, because Anand will be even more abusive if he finds out. So, I have not gone. Pa's fever is not subsiding, you write, but you have still not taken him to the English doctor. Why not, Brother? I sent you the money for that. Do take him soon.

You long to see me; I do too, to see all of you. But even if you had the money, you could not leave Pa in this state. Sometimes, I just want to pack my bags and leave, while Anand is at work. Shall I run away from Mumbai and come home? But then how will I return the money I borrow from my friends here? There is no money to spare at home. Anand will come to the village to drag me back. I'm just a maid to him, a maid to do his laundry and cook his food when he wants to eat at home.

I don't know how long I can stand this prison. The walls are closing in on me, and my world is collapsing. I'm glad, in a way, that we cannot meet. I've changed, Brother. I'm no longer the younger sister you knew. I'm exhausted and drained. Not just physically because of the miscarriage, but emotionally, mentally. I've forgotten what it is to laugh, to joke, to tease. What will it take to bring back the old Surekha, you ask. I need to be loved and cared for, and only my family can do that. My husband is cruel, even though I have done nothing. Yes, I did lose his child, but it was not my fault.

Suresh came to see me one afternoon. I had not seen him since that night at the hospital. He said he could not stay away. He was concerned because I had not come to the centre. I told him everything. The tenderness in his eyes lifted my heart so that I did not want him to leave. I clung to him and sobbed.

Poor fellow, he did not know what to do. Another man's wife crying on his shoulder. I think he has feelings for me, but how can he express them? I'm a married woman. He comforted me and said he would think about my problems, and tell me what, in his opinion, I should do. His mother is looking out for a bride for him. Once he is married, he won't be able to drop by and see me; his wife won't like it.

The tears are coming fast. I don't want them to erase what I have written.

Love,
Surekha

* * *

Respected Ma and Pa,

Greetings from Mumbai! Yes, I have fully recovered from the miscarriage and am quite strong again. Also, I have been eating *jaggery* and ghee with my *roti* as you suggested. You said I should try for another pregnancy as soon as I'm strong to make up for the loss of the baby. I don't know if that ache will ever go away, Ma, but I will try. I also pray every morning and evening.

Anand is busy at work as usual, but he takes good care of me when he is at home. He also calls me two or three times a day to make sure I'm not brooding. My friend, Asha, still brings me food, and keeps me company whenever she can.

I'm glad that Pa is much better, and does not have fever. I miss chatting in the evenings with Pa.

It is difficult to sit alone at home all day long. Anand says that I should not start teaching so soon after losing the baby, so I rest most of the time.

I long to come home and see you all.

Your loving daughter,
Surekha

* * *

Dearest Kamala,

I was so glad to receive your letter. You sound well and happy. You say that your in-laws treat you like their own daughter, and Raju brings you a little gift every evening, even if it is a tiny flower. Hold on to this love, my friend, hold on fast.

You have told Raju everything about me. I understand that, but please make sure he doesn't tell his parents. Thank Raju for suggesting that he can talk to Anand when you both come to Mumbai. They were together for a few years in the village school, after all.

Anand will not change even with a child at home, as you think. Honestly Kamala, I don't know if I am in the frame of mind to go through a pregnancy and take care of a baby. As it is, I go through times when I feel I cannot live like this any longer. What if the baby comes to harm?

I agree that I should keep busy, but how, if Anand won't let me go out and teach?

Kamala, does Raju kiss you and touch you every day? You know what I mean…. How I long for love. Without it, I'm not a woman, not a human being; I'm nothing.

I will wait for your letter. Write soon. Give my best to Raju.
Surekha

* * *

Dearest Brother,

Pack my bags and leave right away, Brother? You want to sell one of our cows so that I can repay Asha or Suresh. My heart surges with joy at the thought of coming home and being with all of you. You write that you will let Ma and Pa know the truth once I decide to leave, and you feel that they too will want me to do that.

Let's think through everything carefully. After the pleasure of meeting wears off, do you think they will want me to stay at home? They will be worried about what everyone will say. They will ask me to go back to my husband, and make peace with him and accept his ways. My in-laws will drag me to their home, and say that I must have driven their son to drinking and women. My coming home will only be a short-term relief. I have to face my life as it is … or not.

Every morning when Anand leaves for work, it is such a relief. I can breathe again. Then Asha drops in in the afternoons. But once the evening shadows begin to lengthen, and the sun goes down, the walls close in on me, I gasp for breath. I pace up and down like a caged animal. Once I rushed out of the house and went to Suresh's office, not caring about the consequences. Sometimes, I just sit in the lobby of the building, and stare into space. I get pitying glances as people return home. Some think I'm crazed; and maybe I am, because a few times I have rushed out onto the street, and walked fast like the traffic rumbling past me. I think about walking into the cars and getting run over. But then I have a scary thought: what if I don't die, but become a cripple? So, I turn around and walk back home, trying to slow down my galloping heart, and covering my ears with my hands to muffle the sound of the traffic, for those sounds only increase the pounding in my head.

As I reach my flat, the pounding becomes fast again. What if Anand has come home early, and beats me up because he thinks that I had gone to Suresh? I turn the key and open the door. Relief washes over me. There is no one; only the demons of my mind. Then, standing in the kitchen, I stuff some food into my mouth; I'm so hungry. Satiated, I lie down on the bed, and the walls begin to close in on me again. I yearn for oblivion as I cry myself to sleep.

I want to be home, Brother. I long to be home.
Surekha.

* * *

Dearest Brother,

I got your letter two days ago. I'm happy that Pa is much better. Thank God, you don't have to spend money on medicines anymore. I know I haven't written for long, but that is because I have nothing new to write about. My life is the same, Anand is the same. I guess, I've been thinking a lot about all of you.

Brother, it's high time you were married. I know that Ma and Pa were waiting till there was more money for you to start a family, but for how long can you wait? Ma is getting older and needs help. And since I'm married, there will be someone else for you and for them. I don't know if ... when I'll see you all again.

Suresh came yesterday to give me his wedding invitation. His bride-to-be is pretty. He was excited when he showed me her photo, told me all about her, and about the wedding preparations. I would love to go, but Anand won't want to. He won't want me to see Suresh; he hates him. When I told Suresh that, and when he saw how pale I was, he sighed. He didn't need to say anything. I knew he was sorry for me. But what can he do? I'll keep the invitation hidden from Anand until the wedding; just in case I can go with Asha, who has also been invited.

That's all for now. I'll write to Ma and Pa tomorrow.
Surekha

* * *

Respected Pa and Ma,

I hope Pa is resting to get his strength back. You must rest too, Ma, as you have stayed up nights with him.

You should find a girl for Brother soon. He is four years older than I am, and still not married. There'll never be enough money, but she will be a help and be a companion for you all.

I don't know if Brother mentioned that I may be able to come home for a while. Once you and Brother approve of a girl, it will just be a matter of a few weeks until the wedding. Unlike Mumbai, where some modern boys and girls take months to get to "know" each other, before they get married. Would that make a happier marriage? I wonder.

I will arrange my visit once the date is fixed. How can Brother be married without me? I would like to be there for my new sister-in-law as well, so that I can help her settle down before I return to Mumbai.

I'm completely recovered now, and am eating well. I know you're waiting for good news from me.

Your loving daughter,
Surekha

* * *

My dear Kamala,

Hope you and Raju are fine. You say that there is a lot of cooking to do, and milking the cows, and other chores; but if you're happy, work feels like play.

Kamala, please help find Brother a nice girl. I know he is lonely without me, and bears the full burden of looking after Ma and Pa. Maybe there is someone in Raju's family. Ours is a small family, so she will not have too many people to worry about.

I will come home for my Brother's wedding. It will be so special.

In your last letter, you were asking about Anand. Nothing has changed, Kamala. I live out each day as it comes, waiting for the day to end and night to fall, so that I can sleep and dream. Dream about what, you ask? I dream of a world where my husband laughs with me and talks to me; we tease one another, fight, and make up. I dream of three little ones running around, and me chasing them with food in my hand. I dream of making lots of quilts and selling them, of teaching young girls and women.

I pray that your dreams come true. Mine will not, not with this man. Perhaps, in another life.

Take care, my friend.

Love,
Surekha

* * *

My dear Brother,

So, you have seen ten girls, and you don't like anyone. Be patient, the right person will come along.

If I run away from Anand, I would have to go where no one can find me. How would I live?

As the date of Suresh's wedding comes closer, my heart sinks. Will we still be friends? Will he care for me like before?

Once again, the monsoons are here with a vengeance. Everything is wet and mouldy. I don't feel like stepping out into rivers of mud, with all the trash floating in them. The windows are constantly foggy and wet with the moisture. My eyes are often full of tears. I see a blurred image of everything, even of myself, in the mirror. It is as if I'm becoming smaller and smaller ... vanishing. Sometimes, when the tears are flowing, the edges of my image are so fuzzy, that it appears as if I have no shape, no features. I'm just a blob. A blob of nothing; no body, no mind, numb, feeling less and less every day. And yet, I know myself. I'm there somewhere. Maybe not in this body, but floating above it. I don't know.

I will be able to see through the windows again when the rains are over. I will be able to see the next building, its tiny, shuttered windows, and the heaps of stinking waste — rotting banana peel, pieces of roti, splattered rice, plastic bags, and other unspeakable things. My mirror will clear too. And when my eyes are dry, that shapeless blob that is Surekha will be no more. There will only be light, sunlight, as it streams in from the window; or, a new image of Surekha will be reflected. Unflinching. Strong. Self-contained.

Brother, I want you to know that I care for all of you deeply. Please let Ma and Pa know that. And I'm sorry for being the cause of so much sadness.

Love always,
Surekha

Ba

❦

"LUNCH IS DONE," Ba said, picking up the newspaper and turning towards the bedroom. She was in the habit of retiring after lunch with the day's newspapers and the novel she was reading. She was seventy-five and I seventeen, but I remember her "quiet time" ever since I was a first-grader. I remember snuggling up to her on weekends after a large family lunch.

I would plead, "Just one more story, Ba, please, before you take a nap."

"Okay, Suneel," she would agree, "then, young man, off you go and play."

When I came home from school around four, she always opened the door for me with a steaming mug of tea in hand. My parents returned from work at seven, and I looked forward to my Ba's warm smile and chatter about what she had been occupied with during the day. "I walked for half an hour before lunch and oh, I saw such beautiful flowers on Bruce street," or, "Did you hear about the accident at the intersection?" She showed me the book she was reading with comments like, "Such trash!" or, "Amazing, you should read it during the holidays." She often went over to our neighbour Susie's house. Susie was eighty-seven and completely bed-ridden. Ba read to her, made her a cup of coffee, chatted, and cheered her up.

Other neighbours greeted her with a warm, "Hello, Mrs.

Mehta," and Ba always stopped to ask about their families and jobs.

When she went out, she would come home and tell us, "Marie's baby is lovely; I saw her at the park today." Or, "Poor Henry, his knee is really bothering him. I told him I would get him the Ayurvedic ointment when I go to India."

I remember being very upset one evening because of a C-grade in a science project, as I usually got an A. I was miserable after a heated discussion with my parents. Ba came into my room later that evening and said, "Suneel, you can't always get an 'A.' A 'C' will motivate you to work harder and not take your strengths for granted."

"You're right, Ba," I replied.

I had wondered about Ba's transformation after my grandfather had passed away about seven years ago. No longer did I hear the tinkling of glass bangles as Ba approached; no longer did I see her in a deep red or green sari with a vermilion bindi on her broad forehead. Those were the days when she was often in the kitchen, making traditional *mithai* that all of us, but especially Dada, loved. Now, I was used to seeing her in a white sari, no bindi, and a single gold bangle on her arm; now, she only helped my mother with the cleaning and chopping of vegetables and rarely went near the stove.

One Friday night when Ba was already asleep, I tiptoed into her room to pick up a book that I had forgotten. I was surprised to see my parents in a whispered discussion by her bedside. I got my book and turned to leave. My dad came out with me. We went to the family room, where he seated me next to him on the sofa.

"Listen, Suneel, Ba has been diagnosed with a lung condition that will make her bed-ridden in about six to eight months. They did some tests as her cough wouldn't go away; we just got the reports this afternoon. She says that she wants to visit India before she gets weak. We don't know when she will leave Toronto; it depends on what the doctors tell her on Tuesday. It could be in two to three weeks. When she returns to us — she wants to be away for about a month and a half —she may be quite ill. So, try to be cheerful and chatty while she is here. You never know what turn the disease will take."

With tears in my eyes I got up and stood by the window, staring at a blurred image of red and yellow tulips that filled our garden outside.

My dad got up as well, put his arm around me, and said, "She has had a wonderful life, Suneel. But all things must come to an end ... these tulips, too, will soon fade away and be replaced by summer flowers."

My mom was crying when I went into the kitchen to get a glass of water. She hugged me tightly and said, "Beta, it is a great shock now, but we will have to accept it. Soon I won't have a mother, but who knows, miracles can happen, and she may be with us longer than we expect."

I was grief-stricken, but managed to talk to Ba as I had before. The following evening, she said, "I'm lucky. It's the mango season in India. Also, your aunt and uncle are making arrangements for me to visit Trimbakeshwar, the famous Shiva temple near Mumbai. I hope I can go to Panchwati as well ... that's where Rama and Sita are supposed to have lived during their years of exile."

"Ba, it's going to be really hot. I remember the sweet mango juice I had the last time we went. What do you want to take for Ajay and Anjali? I'll send some video games for Ajay, and I guess Mom can buy some clothes and make-up for Anjali."

"Yes, I'm sure they'll like that. Your cousins will be so grown up. I can't wait to see them."

On the weekend before she left, my Mom and I helped her pack. She seemed more tired than I had ever seen her before, and I wondered how she would manage the long journey. I packed some books that she wanted to take with her. I put Anita Rau Badami's *Tamarind Mem* in the bag. I said, "Oh, you will enjoy this novel. I've read the reviews. The book has stories of several related women, and how they end up where they are."

Without looking at me she whispered, "Good! I too will be finishing up soon."

A week later, she left. She was very excited at the prospect of meeting friends and relatives in Mumbai. She hadn't been home for over five years. However, when we went to the airport to see her off, there was heaviness in her step and sadness in her eyes, though her lips were constantly smiling. As she turned to go through security, she brushed away her tears and waved a final goodbye.

We drove back home in silence. We were all thinking the same thought — what will her condition be when she returns to Toronto in six weeks?

Those six weeks went by quickly, as I prepared for my final school exams. We tried to speak to Ba about once a week. She always sounded happy. "Hello, Suneel!" she'd shout. Older people always think that the greater the length of the phone line, the louder they have to shout! "Are you studying hard?"

"Yes, Ba. How's the weather out there?"

"Hot and humid ... and I'm enjoying every minute of it. Can you hear the firecrackers? India just won the cricket match against Australia. Did you like the postcards I sent you? Aren't they colourful?"

Her return date was set for a few days after my exams. We filled her room with flowers. My mom cooked her favourite dishes and the house was filled with the sweet smells of cinnamon, cardamom, and saffron, and the aroma of fried *puri* and pungent curries. We drove to the airport in high spirits. The house had seemed rather empty and the family incomplete without her.

We waited outside the arrival gate, peering at the passengers as they went past. Just as we were thinking that perhaps she could not find her bags, an airline attendant walked up to us with Ba in a wheelchair. My mother's eyes widened and my father put his arm around her shoulders. My hand flew to my mouth when I saw wrinkles and sagging flesh that I had not seen before. She seemed to have aged ten years in six weeks. With a wan smile and a far away look, she tried to get up from the wheelchair to get into the car. I quickly grabbed her arm as she swayed and wobbled in front of me. She sat in the back seat with me and grasped my hand. We didn't speak much.

She was out of breath when she said, "It was ... was a good trip ... I'm so glad I went. I ... I may not be able to go again."

My parents took her to the doctor the very next day. The news was not good. The doctor suggested moving her to hospital, or she could die peacefully at home. It would be a matter of weeks or a few months. Ba decided to stay at home.

I vividly remember those long summer days. Ba used to rest in her room most of the time. I would sometimes sit by her side and read to her. I read to her about the war in Iraq, or I read to her from Rohinton Mistry's latest novel, all the while thinking what it would be like without her. On better days she would have her tea in the yard, happy to be outside under the sun with the trees, the grass, and the flowers.

That summer I had a job as a research assistant at a local university. I played a lot of tennis and hung out with my friends. Soon, the leaves started to turn, the days grew shorter, and I was busy preparing to go to university. Ba was hardly eating, and rarely sat out in the garden anymore. Just two weeks before I was due to leave, she was having tea — my mother had to help her hold the mug now — and she asked me to sit with her.

There, beneath the red maple rustling in the breeze, and the cardinals hopping about and chattering, she said, "Suneel, when you ... go to university, work hard, and ... play hard. Oh ... I wish I had had the chance to study ... have fun..." She stopped and had to take a deep breath before she could continue. Her voice was fluttery when she said, "But ... but

... be true to yourself." As I nodded, unable to speak because of the lump in my throat, I noticed the wilting impatiens and the fading marigolds in our yard. The sky had clouded over, the pleasant breeze had turned blustery, and my mom and I helped Ba to her bed.

The next afternoon, the doctor said she was sinking. When my mother woke me up at four thirty in the morning, it was raining heavily after a night of lightening and thunder. I went in to see her, and stood with my parents by my side. She looked very gentle and peaceful. I stroked the back of her small hand, the one that had grasped mine when she returned from India. But now it felt cold, and her skin was more wrinkled and finer than before.

By eight o'clock that morning, when friends had gathered at our home, and we took Ba to the crematorium, I was relieved that the rain had finally stopped. The sky was blue and the sun was breaking through the clouds. The robins and cardinals seemed to have come to the yard to bid a final goodbye to Ba, and as we lowered the stretcher into the hearse, I thought I saw a slight smile at the corners of her mouth.

Some weeks later, I was attending my first classes at university. I was excited about my courses, and I was trying to make friends and get used to being away from home. There were times when I felt very unsure of myself — of my intelligence, my knowledge, and even the values I had grown up with. There was a guy from my dorm who believed in partying every day of the week, but I had to excuse myself often because of an assignment or test. Soon he stopped asking me, and gave me a hard, cold look if we happened to meet.

And then there were the drugs and the alcohol. It was difficult to stay away from those things and admit it, when many other students bragged about what they had tried, and how often.

It was at times such as these that Ba's face swam before my eyes, and I remembered her last words to me. Those words never failed to encourage me in moments of doubt and wavering confidence — they helped me draw upon an inner strength that I never knew I possessed.

The Scent of Mogra

❧

AH ... THE SCENT OF MOGRA from an incense stick. I, Sushmita, am in the world of the dead. But this fragrance transports me back to a red swing on Earth, to mogra flowers, to a breeze carrying their musky scent, to our old home in Ahmedabad, on the banks of the Sabarmati river, near the Hanuman temple. I hear the ringing of the temple bells fade away in the distance. What is that sound? Tina, my little daughter Tina, calling, "Mama! Mama!"

Wait. I see another image. I see Megha and she has red flowers in her hair. But who is she? She is in the woods with her friends, chasing away the monkeys who steal the mangoes that they are trying to knock down from the trees with stones. She has gathered a few in her velvet *odhani*, the colour of *sindhur,* which she wraps tightly around her shoulders. Oh! Is she Tina? An earlier incarnation, Tina?

"Mama! Mama!"

Tina comes out to the verandah, and plunks herself on the swing. She pushes the swing hard to make it go faster, but I am dizzy and can easily overpower a five-year-old to bring it to a slow stop. I take her hand and we get off the swing. To distract her, I lead her to the mogra flowers and together we inhale their fragrance.

"Let's make a garland with them for Lord Krishna," I tell her. She nods energetically and starts to pluck with her little fingers. We sit down on the swing again with the flowers in my sari *pallu*. The white flowers glow like pearls as I pour them between us onto the red swing. I thread the flowers as Tina hands them to me one by one.

The incense stick with the mogra fragrance is burnt out. In this place, I don't know where I can find another. I left twenty years ago, in Earthly time. Tina must have been around forty then. She had come from her home abroad to see me when I was in hospital. She would sit with me and stroke my hand. She would tell me about her two children, my grandsons. I tried to listen, to understand, but I was already far away. And when I was alert, I was anxious about leaving my husband Ramesh behind; he was seventy-eight. How would he manage without me? The best thing was to take him with me where I went. But not at the same time. That would be too much for everyone to cope with — our two sons and Tina. So, I went alone. I was scared. The pain had been too much. I couldn't breathe. Each breath I took seemed to be the last; there was so much effort.

But I passed over easily. What a big deal everyone makes about death. I saw my family weeping. My son's daughter, Diya, came to the hospital room, looked at my body on the bed, and ran out, sobbing. Poor child, she was only thirteen at the time.

Tina's childhood was happy and very special to me, maybe because she was my youngest. Some episodes from that time unfold before me now, as if it were only yesterday that they happened.

* * *

"Where are you going? Where are you going? I want to put it on too," Tina said, sticking out her hand. My red nail polish still wet, I painted the little nail on her index finger. She looked up at me and smiled, eyes shining. She trailed after me as I went into the bedroom to get ready for a dinner party we had to go to. I laid out a black sari with a red border. Red. The colour of red robins. I remembered them from several years ago, when we were living in Kenya. They liked to visit our garden in Nairobi, hopping about the vegetable patch when I went to get the sweet green squash that was ready to be picked. They twittered on the steps that led to the front door where Tina played, or when she was squatting over a piece of old newspaper because I was trying to toilet train her. "Red, red!" she called out. I ran over from the kitchen to see if it was blood from her bowels. Ah, no, it was only the robins twittering, and she, my little one, talking back to them.

Now there is smoke here, and it fills the air with another smell. Is it an incense stick? I don't see any. It is a smell I know. It used to make me cough. But I have not smelled it for over twenty years, not since I came here. It will come to me in a minute, it's so familiar ... cigarettes! How can I forget that terrible smell? I didn't think I would smell it in this world; thank God, it's clearing up now. My husband was a chain smoker for many years, until the doctors scared him. Your lungs will collapse, they said. So, he quit at that very moment. What a man. He didn't smoke again, ever. Not a puff. A man made of stony determination, and a loving family man.

I took him away exactly one month after I passed over. Pulled him over so that he wouldn't be a burden on anyone, so that he wouldn't be miserable. Why exactly a month later, you ask? Easy for everyone to remember the dates. Better for him not to live on after I left him alone. Yes, it was traumatic for the children. Tina was back in Canada when she got the news. She was angry.

She asked him, "Why did you too leave me?"

He, a grumpy voice in her head, told her, "What can I do? Mummy came to get me. She took me away."

I saw Tina when she was driving in Toronto, just a few months after Ramesh and I had passed over. She'd had to stop on the side of the road because she imagined being in a car crash, dying, and then immediately meeting us. She panicked and felt that she could not breathe; losing both parents within a month of each other was too much to deal with.

There are times when we can look down and see what's going on in the world that we left, and in the lives of our near and dear ones, but not always. What is going on in Tina's life? She is sad, I know. I see her weeping. I see her praying. She even asks us, her father and me to help her. Can we, from a different world, help Earthly beings? For twenty years, I've never thought about it, but Tina is confused, upset. Why can't I see the cause of her pain? We used to talk about the mysteries of life on earth, but life in this place is even more baffling.

Though I died more than two decades ago, I have not been back on Earth even once. I have seen other people here go back and return several times. You may be wondering what I'm talking about when I speak of being back in the world after death. If you are born a Hindu, you are told that we all have many lives to live. The cycle of birth and death will stop only when we have reached a high spiritual state. Those who had led a "good" life would have fewer and better lives to live, until finally, there are no more births to go through.

My life was simple; I did what I was supposed to do. Ramesh and I had some very good times. I have already told you that we lived in Africa, but we also moved to different cities within India. I never complained to my husband about moving so much — from countries, cities, or homes. I was content with life as it was.

Whenever my husband or children needed me, I was always there for them. Soon after I had passed over, I heard my doctor tell my son that I was one of the most courageous patients he'd ever had. I don't think that was anything big, really. I simply did what I was asked to do by the doctors, and I didn't whine and grumble because I had to bear what was to be borne. Complaining would have only aggravated the people around me, the people who were doing the best they could for me.

As a bank manager, Ramesh could have made pots of money by taking bribes, but he never did. I did not mind that we could not afford expensive holidays, or that I could not buy much jewellery. He lived by the motto, "honesty is the best policy." And Tina has taken this lesson to heart.

Telling you about my life, about my husband and my daughter, has taken me back to our flat in Mumbai.

The rain had finally stopped, and I opened the windows. The sea looked calmer, but the breeze was humid. The smell of cinnamon and saffron wafted in. It reminded me of the sweet rice dish which I always made for my birthday. Wouldn't it be a nice surprise for my husband if I made it even though it was not my birthday? I went to the kitchen and started the preparations. Tina came to see how to make it. Whether she was busy studying for exams, or preparing to teach college students, she sometimes liked to relax by cooking; she wanted to make something different, something new. That youngest child of mine was creative.

I know now that she thinks of me often. I can see that she writes stories, and some of the characters she creates are based on me. I didn't realize that I had such an impact on her, for it was her father with whom she had intellectual conversations. I guess, because I did not go to college, we didn't talk about serious things. But we did spend time together, and what did we talk about? Oh, new recipes, what I saw at the bazaar, about our friends and relatives. She would tell me about her colleagues and her students. Then she would pick up a book to read. She was always reading novels. Sometimes, she would tell me a little of the story, and say, "What do you think she should do? Should the heroine leave home, or stay and make the best of things?"

"But where would she go?" I would ask.

"She would have to be courageous, earn money, and lead her own life. It's better than putting up with hypocrisy," she would say.

"It's more difficult than it sounds." I would then get up to make tea, and bring her a cup before she started grading papers.

When Tina was in elementary school, I would buy her books like *Cinderella, Snow White and the Seven Dwarfs,* and would tell her stories about kings and queens, and palace intrigues. I changed the stories a little each time, and that fired Tina's imagination. I would also recite nursery rhymes that I had learned at school.

She was growing up fast though, and started spending more time with her brother. But I think that I did instill in her a love of words.

I feel as if I am aloft a current of air that is gently pushing me along. I see a light ahead. It doesn't hurt my eyes, though. It is bright, but soft. Maybe I'm about to be born again. No, I'm still in the world of the dead. Is it what we called heaven? For it is full of light and fragrant air; there is mellifluous music, and when the breezes touch me softly, I overflow with love and joy.

***

"Princess Megha! Come back, it's time for your *sarangi* lesson." Her lady-in-waiting, Gangabai, is running towards her, and she lets go of her friend's hand as she turns to leave. Her father, the *maharaja*, will be angry if she is late for her lesson. She enjoyed playing the *sarangi*. She also loved to listen to her other tutors talking about distant lands, their myths and legends. Her friends were not as lucky, either because they were the children of lesser courtiers, or because their fathers were not liberal enough to let their daughters study.

But which life am I describing? I had started talking about my life with Ramesh and Tina; it was the scent of mogra from an incense stick that set me off. Megha's life as a princess is, I think, one of Tina's previous lives. Perhaps, it unfolds before me for a special reason; perhaps, it will give me an insight into Tina's suffering.

"Megha, you have to understand that you're growing up. We must find a match for you. You're almost seventeen." The *maharaja* said. The *rani*, her mother, was there too, nodding in agreement. Megha had been downcast ever since she had heard that a young prince from a neighbouring state was coming in two weeks, with his parents, to see her. Now she looked down, twisting the satin ribbon with which her plaits were tied around her index finger.

"I don't want to get married yet, I want to live with you," she said. "I want to study more, I want to learn dancing, and I want to play with my friends at court." Her mother smiled, but her father was not amused.

"Child, it's time to grow up and live in the real world. Prince Uday is a bright young man, a brave soldier, and very fond of music. You will like him."

"But what will I do if I can't have my tutors, if I can't be with my friends?"

"You will have enough to keep you busy with family and social responsibilities," replied her mother.

Her father said, "No more discussion. Make sure you're ready to greet them when they arrive next week." Megha spent the rest of that day playing soulful melodies on the *sarangi*.

The next week, when Prince Uday and his family arrived, their palace was decorated with mogra flowers and incense, and there was music everywhere. Once all the welcome rituals were performed, and the guests were finally seated, Megha was asked to enter the sitting room. Her mother came to get her. Megha was dressed up in a new silk *ghaghara,* and bedecked with gold and pearls. The queen told her daughter to keep her eyes cast down, and not to look at their guests straight in the eye, as she usually did when she was spoken to. But she quickly stole a glance at Prince Uday, who was looking at her. He smiled when he caught her glance. Well, at least, he doesn't seem to be the grim and stuffy sort, she thought. And within a matter of days, her marriage was fixed up.

It was such a relief when Tina's marriage was fixed up. She was twenty-eight, and we thought that she would remain un-married. She was so caught up with her teaching career and college life, and she didn't seem to be particularly interested in anything else. She was going to be far away, all the way in Canada, and we didn't know anyone there. When I got married at seventeen, I only moved from Ajmer to Ahmedabad.

Prince Uday was such a charming man —bright, articu-late, and well-read. Megha enjoyed being with him and was falling in love. It was a joyful time in her life. Of course, she missed her home, her friends, parents, and tutors. But Uday was a wonderful teacher. They had different musicians come and play for them almost every evening. Women found him handsome and exciting, and Megha felt her first twinges of jealousy. Sometimes there was dancing, and even the dancers looked at her husband. But then Uday always looked at her and smiled in that special way that made her heart melt, and she brushed aside her jealousy, even if she thought that he was returning their glances. On some other evenings, it would be just him and Megha in the sitting room. He would read from new books that he had ordered ... history, poems, or stories. She cherished this time with him.

In their second year of marriage, she was with child. Uday and his family were thrilled. He treated her with such gentleness. There would be an heir to the throne. His father, the *mahara-jah,* was old and unwell, and there was talk of him handing over his kingdom to his son. Megha would be a *rani.* Would Uday then be able to spend time with her as he did now? But, she thought, she too would be busy with the baby, and with her duties as a queen.

It was a girl. All the pampering and tenderness suddenly stopped. Uday seemed excited about being a father, but Megha could see that he was covering up his disappointment that it was not a son. Some of her in-laws looked at her almost dis-dainfully, as if to say she was not capable of producing a son.

Though Megha didn't think Uday believed that, she felt some tenseness creep into his interactions with her. Nor did he have the time any more to read with her, as he was weighed down by important matters of state. His father participated less as each day went by. Sometimes, Uday returned to their chambers so late that Megha was already fast asleep.

But the joy of Megha's life was her little daughter, the princess Yamini. She had large dark eyes and a mop of black hair. She was fair with rosy cheeks and a ready smile on her face. She was alert, and seemed to notice every little thing, especially a change in her mother's moods. Megha often thought that the baby would speak to her if she could, for her eyes spoke volumes, and she seemed to understand every nuance of what Megha felt.

Then one day Uday told her curtly that they were at war with her father's kingdom, and that she was not to communicate with friends or family in her home state in any way whatsoever. "What?" she said. "I'm to go home next month with Yamini. They haven't even seen her yet."

"You cannot go now. There is no way that I will send a child of mine to the enemy."

"You forget that the enemy is my family, and your child's grandparents."

"You cannot go, Megha. Unfortunately, this is a state matter." Uday's tone was softer now.

And that was that. She longed to be with her parents. She wasn't allowed to go there for her delivery as was customary, for Uday's parents wanted their grandchild to be born in their palace. She wondered for how long the war would continue, and when she would be able to go home.

Home. I made homes in so many cities, just like Tina. How did you manage this, you ask? A good question. Yes, it drains you both physically and emotionally to live in different places, and then pack up and leave again, just when the unfamiliar has become familiar, just when you feel that you now know people you can talk to. I, of course, was happy being a housewife, but Tina could not have a career because of all their moving about. They moved from Toronto to London, to Singapore, then Mumbai, and back to Toronto. A very disruptive life. But enriching at the same time. Everywhere they moved she tried to find something meaningful to do and enjoyed it. She thought of herself only after the children were settled and the house was set up. It's high time though she starts to think of herself first, now that the children have grown up; this is her time.

The war was about a narrow tract of land between the two kingdoms, a piece of land with rich soil. Each side claimed it for itself. *What a thing to fight over and cause so much anguish for me*, Megha thought. She hadn't seen her parents for so long. Uday was hardly spending time with her, and she was lonely without real friends. It was almost three years since her marriage, and instead of being closer to one another, she and Uday were drifting apart. He wasn't particularly interested in the child, and didn't have much of a relationship with her. Every evening he was busy, or so he said. Busy with what? Megha would ask. And he would mumble something about the affairs of the state, the war, and so on. And then he stopped coming to her bed, using Yamini as an excuse. He didn't want to be woken up by her. He needed a good night's rest for all the hard work he put in during the day. Though Yamini hardly woke up in the nights now.

The worst can never happen to me, we all think, and when it does we are totally unprepared. Megha found out that Uday had taken up with a dancing girl. *I'm still so young*, she thought. *Why does he need a concubine?* Megha confronted him the same evening. Uday just shrugged his shoulders, and said, "I'm a man, a prince, and it is normal to have a mistress. I'm taking care of you, and you are my queen. I can seek my pleasures elsewhere if I want."

Megha said, "But I love you and I thought you loved me.

Why don't you ever come to my bed? Why don't we spend time together, reading, talking, as we used to do?" Uday raised his eyebrows and left the room.

The years passed. Uday's parents passed away and princess Yamini became a young woman. She was better educated than her mother. Megha had made sure of that. But she fell in love with her tutor, and wanted to marry him. Uday brought suitors to the palace, young men from noble families, some highly educated, and others who had seen the world. Yamini was adamant. Megha tried to reason with her, as mother and daughter had a close bond.

Megha thought of her daughter as a friend. She was the love of her life, as she had lost the love of her husband. Yamini was an only child, and though she had a few friends, she was closer to her mother than to any of them. She had grown up seeing the distance between her parents, and her mother's melancholy, and so now she refused to marry someone "suitable" and risk not being loved. Megha secretly empathized with her daughter. Finally, late one evening, she sent her off with money and jewels to be with her love, when Uday was in the arms of his mistress. There was great confusion and feverish activity, when in the morning, the princess was missing. Megha participated in the outcry, and then the search. In the meantime, Megha had received news that her daughter was safely on her way to a place far away from her father's kingdom, and would soon be married to the man she loved, in the presence of his parents. Megha hoped they would love her like a daughter. Megha cried her heart out, not because Yamini was missing as the others thought, but because she had no companion to lighten the burden of her lonely life.

Megha, as her life unfolds before me, reminds me of Tina, as she grew up from a little girl to a mother of two sons. Perhaps, Tina is unhappy just as Megha was, for the same reasons. Has she then not finished with unfaithful or unsuitable husbands? Or does she have to live through this over many lifetimes?

Perhaps, it is a lesson she has not yet learned — to let go, to seek contentment within herself.

Tina had often thought of what it would be like to live in another age, a period far back in history. How exciting it would be to be part of Emperor Akbar's court! But if she had been there in yet another life, she may have also experienced deep loss. So often, the same problems follow women across generations, across cultures; a princess in Emperor Akbar's court in the sixteenth century may have been betrayed by her prince, just as now, my Tina feels the anguish of her husband's infidelity. And we have seen Megha, somewhere between those two eras, suffering in the same way. And ironically, it is sometimes women who perpetuate injustices against women; whether it is the cruel mother-in-law, or other women who cast their spell on men. Tragedies and disillusionments cling to women like dark shadows, never letting go. To be free, the victims must change, must grow. I see Tina growing now, growing in a spiritual sense, nurturing the strength within her. Just as Megha did after Yamini left, while Uday led an increasingly decadent life.

Many months after Yamini was married, Uday found her whereabouts. Knowing that she was happy and with child, he decided to leave her be. It would be worse to bring the matter out into the open, drag her back home, and make his family a target of jibes and sneers. His reputation, thankfully, Megha thought, was more important to him than his daughter, and so she would be left in peace. Nobody ever found out about Megha's part in Yamini's escape. And since Uday and Megha led separate lives, Megha could visit her daughter from time to time and see her grandchildren. If Uday knew that Megha was away for short periods of time, he did not care. When she went, she took with her gifts for her son-in-law's family, and especially for her grandchildren. She was made to feel very welcome, and mother and daughter spent long hours together talking. Megha attempted to help with the household chores

Yamini had to do, though Megha had never lifted a finger before in her life. She, however, was good with the children, and got them ready for school on time. In the evenings, when Yamini was preparing dinner, Megha would sit with the two boys and the little girl, and tell them stories from her childhood, and about their mother when she was a child, and the three pairs of eyes would shine with fascination. When it was time for Megha to return home after a visit that often lasted a couple of weeks, her grandchildren begged her to tell them when she would come again.

I visited Tina for a couple of weeks when they were living in London. I played with my youngest grandchild. The cough I had developed in Mumbai before coming to London persisted, though Tina gave me different cough syrups. They seemed to help for a while, but the cough always returned. A month after returning to Mumbai, I had bad news; I had a disease that filled my lungs with mucus. I had less than a year to live. Little did I know when I was in London that it would be the last time I would see my daughter's children. The other bad news was that Tina and her family would return to Canada soon, and so be further away from Mumbai.

Megha spent the time between visits ordering gifts and clothes for her grandchildren. She had taken up playing the *sarangi* again. A court musician oversaw her progress. It was a surprise that she had not forgotten what she had learned as a young girl in her father's palace, and with practice, it all came back to her. Her parents were still alive. The war with her husband's state had left her father's fortune depleted, and her father looked old beyond his years. Now that the war was over, she could visit her parents and she went often. She loved to meet her childhood friends and talk with them about their lives. Sometimes, when it was possible for Yamini to get away, she came to her grandparents with the children.

We were not there for Tina when they moved to Mumbai; we had already passed over. She felt that keenly. We could have spent some golden moments with our grandchildren, but it was not to be. Fortunately, Tina has fond memories of my parents. When Tina was little, she would come with me when I visited them. She would sit next to her grandfather and play with his short silver hair. "Your hair feels like a hair brush," she would say to him. My father would look at her with his twinkling grey eyes and laugh. When Tina finished school with high grades, my father gave her a red and white batik sari and a small statue of the goddess Sarasvati, the goddess of learning. For years, Tina would not part with these gifts.

Tina's sons do not have such memories of us. Now she hopes that she will be a part of her grandchildren's life when her sons get married. Megha was lucky, that she was so loved by Yamini's children. That made her life bearable, and slowly she ceased to care what her husband did. Will Tina find love in the form of her grandchildren? We all hope to love and be loved in return during our short time on Earth.

When Uday passed over, Megha was sad that her marriage had been a failure and she mourned for him for some time. Uday's nephew became the next *maharajah,* and was very considerate of his aunt, and of his cousin, Yamini. Megha continued to have her own quarters in the palace, and now that Uday was no more, Yamini and her husband could visit with the children during the holidays. And Megha had never been happier. She found fulfillment in teaching her grandchildren, in arranging music lessons for her granddaughter, and martial arts lessons for her two grandsons. She followed their progress avidly, and discussed the lessons with the tutors. As for herself, Megha studied the scriptures, and had a teacher come in to discuss difficult points with her. Finally, now that she was almost fifty, she felt that she was leading a full and happy life.

Joy and sorrow are a part of what it means to be human. The trick is to "treat those two impostors just the same" as Rudyard Kipling said in his poem "If." Tina read the poem out loud to me when she was in college. Some people achieve a degree of equilibrium, and then they are the happier for it.

In her last years, Megha detached herself from her life with Uday. The joys and sorrows of her life now were focused on her daughter and her family. Her nephew, occasionally, came to her for advice. India was on the verge of Independence from the British, and then the princely states would become a part of the Republic of India. Yamini's husband had died prematurely in an accident, and she and her children were living in Megha's part of the palace, with the *maharajah*'s permission. After Independence, he wanted to turn his palace into a hotel. He would keep a small section for himself, but what about Megha, Yamini, and her children? They would have to find an apartment close to the children's school. Yamini would find work as a teacher. And Megha would live out her days in the company of her daughter and grandchildren, surrounded by love and the warmth of family.

I'm floating somewhere like a feather. I'm not where the incense was burning and where the fragrance of mogra filled the air. I'm in a different place, and a soft breeze is pushing me along, though I don't have any sense of movement. It seems like I've been here forever, but no, it's not forever; I'm born again.

* * *

A woman with grey hair, wearing a white-and-red *kurta*, approaches the stage on which I'm seated and climbs up. I have just finished talking to a room full of about sixty people. The perfume from the strands of mogra flowers that decorate the stage has intensified. I'm hot, but I feel exhilarated by the energy of the people who are now leaving; hopefully, more at peace after listening to a talk on the Hindu scriptures and a short meditation session. She covers her head with a red *dupatta*. Who is this? I know this lady. Maybe, she has come to my talks before. She bows down with folded hands before me. I'm not thirty yet, and I feel uncomfortable when older people do that. She looks up into my eyes and smiles. She says,

"Mataji" (mother, that's what I'm called by my "followers" though I would have preferred it if they called me by my name, Sunanda), "I really was inspired by your talk. I would like a mantra from you that I could chant every day and whenever I'm disturbed."

There is something about her ... she is at least seventy-five.... I can't speak for a few long moments, but just stare into her eyes. Whose voice is this? Why does it sound so familiar? And then she says again, "Mataji, so sorry to disturb you."

"Oh no, you are not disturbing me. It's just that I thought I had met you before. Yes, I'll give you the mantra that will bring peace into your life and to everyone close to you. Will you come to the lecture next week? I will give it to you then."

She says, "This is my first time here. And, yes, I'll be here next week." She hesitates, then adds, "You know, I feel that I know you too. You remind me of my mother, though you are so young. My mother passed on many, many years ago, of course."

With hands folded together in a *namaste,* she bows to me once again, and moves away to make place for the next person in line waiting to see me. I know who she is now. My eyes follow Tina until she reaches the door. Her red *dupatta* slips down the back of her head, revealing shoulder-length hair gleaming silver in the brightly illumined hall. She takes her coat from the rack and buttons it up to her chin. She quickens her pace, smiling, as she thinks of meeting her grandchildren soon, for dinner. Then she walks out into a chilly fall evening in Toronto.

No Other Way

❧

"**S**LUT!**"** RAJ SHOUTED when Mira walked in the door. He had come home from Udaipur a day early because he had travelled in his associate's horse carriage. His face was red with anger and alcohol too, Mira suspected. "Where were you?" he demanded.

"I went to meet a friend who has just had a baby." Mira hastily covered her head with her sari *pallu*. Of course, she couldn't tell Raj that she had gone to see her Roma friend Shanti, in the Dom encampment, and her new born baby, Syeira.

"I don't care. You should be home when I'm home." He shoved her aside and stalked out of the room.

Mira lay down with her eyes closed, trying to calm her heaving chest. As her breathing slowed, she tried to grasp what was happening. She thought about what a family friend had told her soon after their wedding: Raj had been a sickly boy who was teased by his classmates. Maybe, as Shanti had said, his bullying was only a cover up. But she realized now that it had become a part of his character.

The hair on the back of Mira's neck stood on end as she felt again the sting of Raj's slap on her cheek when she had tried to talk to him about his coming home drunk and as she heard in her head echoes of his gruffness every time he spoke with her.

Something within her snapped. The blood pounded against her temples making them throb. She sat up and said aloud, "That's it, I'm leaving. I won't take this anymore."

Mira had told Shanti and her husband, Kailash, that life at her in-law's place was becoming intolerable. Her friends were worried for her, especially since they would soon be leaving Jaisalmer to travel to Persia. It was then that they suggested she could run away with them. However, Kailash had to get permission from the tribe elders, and Mira had to be sure that she could bear the hardship of the travelling Dom, and that probably, she would never be able to return to Jaisalmer. How could she, who had grown up in luxury, live with the poor nomads, sleep on the hard wagon floor, and eat dry roti with nothing more than chillies and onion?

Now Mira paced up and down the room, rubbing the goose bumps on her arms. *How can I leave my parents? How can I leave my home?* she thought. *Even if the elders agree to my going with them, I can't put Shanti and Kailash through this.*

Mira had told her parents before the marriage was finalized that she did not like what little she had seen of Raj. He was thirty and she only fifteen; he looked grumpy, had bloodshot eyes, and a pot belly. But her parents had assured her that it was a good family, and that Raj's parents had approved of her. In any case, she had no say in any decisions about her own life.

If only I had been born in another time, or in a different country where girls are more educated, can work, and choose who they want to marry. Like some of the English women I've seen. Mira also remembered the stories that the tutor at her parents' home had brought for her to read; the story about a girl called Indulekha who fell in love with her cousin, and that of Yamuna, a widow, who ran away from her father-in-law's house and got married again. These heroines had a lot of courage and didn't care about what people thought of them. Could she be like them?

There was a soft knock before Gulab came in with a cup of tea. Her hands were still black from the coal *sigadi*. She had heard Raj shouting and walking out, and rushed in to comfort

Mira as soon as she could. She felt protective towards her young mistress. When Gulab patted her and said, "Drink this, you'll feel better," Mira broke down. In between her sobs, she told her everything. After all, Gulab had looked after her since she was a baby, and had come with her to her husband's house when she got married.

Alarmed by Mira's plan of running away with the Dom, she said, "You will put yourself and them into danger. You must think properly before you take such a drastic step. But if they do agree to let you go with them, I will help you in every way I can." Gulab's green glass bangles tinkled when she pointed to herself. She said, "I too will leave this house once you're gone."

The next day, Mira visited her parents. Her mother said, "Beti, how are you? We were wondering why we haven't seen you for several weeks. Raj must keep you busy. I'm sure you feel settled now that you are more used to one another."

Before she could reply, her father hobbled in with his walking stick. He said, "Raj came to my office today for some business. He said that you are well and happy."

"Liar," Mira muttered under her breath. To her father she said, "We're fine. But how is your knee? It still seems to be bothering you." She left quickly after that. She could not bear to be questioned about her life with Raj. Though she had been married to him for only a few months, it seemed much longer. She felt satisfied that though her parents were aging, they were in good spirits and were well looked after.

If she missed this opportunity to leave, she would be stuck with Raj forever. *Am I being brave or foolhardy?* she wondered. *Once I leave, there is no turning back. And where would I go even if I could return?*

She loved and trusted Shanti and Kailash, though she had met them barely two years ago. She was walking past the encampment close to her parents' house when a girl, about the same age as her, had stopped her to ask for directions to the Jaisalmer market. The Dom group had recently arrived in the city. Mira had been taken with Shanti's vivacious dark eyes, and the friendship between the two had developed quickly. Of course, Mira's parents did not know anything about this; they would have frowned upon their daughter befriending a poor, lowly Dom girl. Subsequently, she had met Kailash, and had thought how lucky Shanti was to have such a man.

If she went with them, she was sure they would care for her, whatever happened. But she couldn't live with them forever. The tribe would never allow her to stay. And how would she escape? She was crazy to even think about it. She didn't know of anyone who had run away, let alone a woman. And, running away with some tribals? They would send out a search party when she did not come home.

Soon after her wedding, she had told her parents about Raj's drinking and his beatings, but they had only said that things would get better once Raj was used to being married. In any case, she had to adjust. Raj's family was well-regarded and it was her duty to preserve the family honour; both his and theirs.

Should she talk to her parents again? Should she ask them to take her back? They wouldn't do that. To take a married daughter back would be unthinkable for them. She was angry with her parents, but when she was calmer, she realized that these were the customs they had grown up with. They only wanted her happiness and knew no other way. But, she wasn't happy.

She must be brave and leave, or she would surely die in this house. Her heart was hammering against her chest as if it would burst. She decided to tell Shanti and Kailash that her mind was made up if they were willing to take the risk. Then, they would think of a plan together.

* * *

The next evening Mira slipped out to the encampment to meet Shanti and Kailash. She found them in their wagon, and told them of her decision.

"You so brave," Shanti said and hugged Mira, while Kailash stood by the door. Then she held Mira at arm's length, looked at her face, and deep into her eyes. She said, "Mira, 'ave you thought about this carefully?"

Mira nodded.

Shanti said again, "You sure you can do this? Leave your parents, leave Jaisalmer, for ever?"

When Mira nodded again, she saw that Shanti's eyes were shining with wonder and admiration. "I don't know if this is courage or cowardice," Mira said. "I can't fight Raj and his family, and so I must run away. And just think of what I will make my parents go through. I feel terrible, but if I don't go with you, I may never get another chance to change my life."

The faraway look in her eyes was replaced by one that searched her friends' faces. "But I'm only thinking about myself," she said. "Have you spoken to the others? And thought about the danger?"

Shanti sat down on the quilt, and Kailash ran his fingers through his long thick hair. He said, "Yes, it'll be dangerous. You with us. We'll 'ave to plan everything, so that you aren't caught when we leave Jaisalmer. And so we aren't caught. We did talk to the elders last night. They said no right away. But then Shanti told 'em about your life, your problems. So now they 'ave changed. But they worry about what 'ould happen to us ... if you're caught."

He paused to look down at his bare feet. Then smiling at Mira, he said, "You 'ave done magic on 'em. I was surprised. Our people, very suspicious. But the elders, the women, talk about how often you come to visit us before marriage. You didn't look down on us like those ... horrible ... mean people. You help when Shanti was expecting; she couldn't do all the chores. And you help when older women couldn't carry heavy tubs of water, hang out clothes to dry. Women want to help you now. And I've promised the men that we'll 'ave good plan."

Kailash moved away from the wagon door, and stood by the window. Mira was trembling and sat down on the quilt next to Shanti. She looked at Syeira, now three weeks old, asleep on her mother's lap. The elders had agreed, and so now she could run away, she thought. Her heart fluttered, unsure of whether to sink in fear, or lift with relief. She couldn't stop twisting the diamond ring around her index finger. She told herself, *I must get it tightened before I leave.*

Finally, she asked, "But what will your families think?"

"That long time away. Who knows what'll happen? Now ...then? We'll meet our families only when we reach Persia," Shanti said. Their families, with the rest of the clan, were already on their way, and had left Kailash and Shanti to help the elderly prepare for the long journey.

Kailash said, "Okay, the elders tell me ... sometimes, we 'ave outside people. They remember children living with 'em ... for months. They remember a man tagging along till one day he go away."

He looked out of the window at the old men sitting down for an after-dinner smoke. He then sat down on the floor across from Shanti and Mira. He said, "You 'ave made difficult decision to leave. No house, no home. It'll be hard for you. We move place to place. Only simple food, only this wagon. But look like your mind made up. I'll tell the elders. They want to know how you escape. Our families ... that'll be after many months."

With tears in her eyes Mira looked at Shanti by her side, and then at Kailash. She swallowed hard. "You will be my family from now on, and I will do my best to become a part of your community. I may not understand everything, I may not do everything right, but I will always be grateful to you for sheltering me." She paused to wipe her eyes with an embroidered handkerchief. "The plan ... the e-escape ... if I'm found out before we leave the city limits, my life is finished. I've heard that the guards often stop the Dom wagons, and search them for stolen goods, and even stolen children. If I'm brought back ... God help me ... R-Raj would beat me, and ... and lock me up forever. I would never be allowed to meet anyone again. And I can't even imagine what they would do to you and your group."

"Only way is to make you like ... us," Kailash said.

"Yes," Shanti agreed. "I'll give you skirt, blouse and scarf. Don't wear gold necklace and diamond earrings. Just beads and silver trinkets."

"But what if they search our wagon and ask who I am?" Mira said.

"We tell 'em that you my sister. Your husband left early with others. You stay behind because you sick. That okay?" said Shanti.

"I'll have to darken my skin somehow, to pass off as your sister," Mira said.

"You two decide all details. We leaving in two weeks. Oh, I better finish work on ol' Shandar's wagon. Also, I must round up all men. Tell 'em this plan." Kailash left. His anxiety was palpable. Mira knew that her decision to go with them had more than doubled the burden he was carrying.

"Bring everything. You sell on the way. You can wear your saris when we far away. No one recognize you. I learn to wear sari too," Shanti giggled, her hand covering her mouth. "You wear my *ghaghara* till then."

Mira said, "I will have to do that, or else I will look different."

Eyeing Mira's bust and arms, Shanti said, "I open up few blouses, so they fit you. Mira, we be together ... we have so much time to talk. But I scared ... be sure you not caught," Shanti sighed loudly, her arms across her chest, hugging herself.

Mira spent many sleepless nights thinking about what she was about to do. She imagined her father dying of shock, of herself shrieking when she was shut up in a tiny room, never to be let out again. When she did doze off fitfully, she dreamt that she was wandering about a wasteland, alone and lost. Then she woke up with a start, and had to suppress a scream rising to her throat. Her relatives and friends saw the dark circles under her eyes and smiled. They said, "So Raj is keeping you awake at night. When are you going to give us the good news?" She learned not to answer this, but to smile and look away.

When there was less than a week to go before her escape, Mira was calm. She was happier than she had ever been since her marriage. She no longer cared about Raj's behaviour. Her parents were lulled into thinking that she had finally settled down. She spent time playing with her ten-year-old brother. She had to hide her tears from him when it dawned on her that she would never see him grow up. He looked up to her. What would he think of his Didi when he understood what she had done?

Gulab promised to get her an herbal powder to darken her skin. She would cover up for her until the evening, by which time the wagons should be outside the city walls. Mira gave Gulab a gold bangle to thank her for all she had done for her ever since she was a baby, and for her friendship and help during these last miserable months. She packed her jewellery in several pouches for easier safe-keeping. She needed to take everything she had, to sell for cash. Her eyes fell upon the tiny diamond studs she had worn as a toddler. They shone like new in their red velvet box, and they would be perfect for Syeira after a few months.

It was at this time when Mira's mind was firm about her decision, when the plan was in place, and she was getting ready to leave, that she felt a tug at her heart; a yearning for love and romance that she had not experienced in her brief marriage. She thought about the sweet romance between Kailash and Shanti, and their love for Syeira. She felt a maternal stirring within her, and she realized that she cared deeply for their child.

At that moment, she was struck by the possibility that there could be a new life growing within her. She felt weak at the knees and sank down on her bed, her hand on her stomach. She had submitted to Raj's lust countless times, for that was all it was, without a shred of affection. If she was pregnant, how would she support a child, while living with the Dom? How would she feel towards it? But, she consoled herself, it was only a possibility, and she wasn't going to complicate her life further by thinking about it for now. She had to push the thought away and just focus on her escape.

The day finally arrived. Raj left while she was still in bed, pretending to be asleep. As soon as she heard him leave she got up, and looked out of the window to watch him walk away. He turned his head to look back; maybe he had felt her watching him. She stood there long after he had disappeared from view. In spite of the winter chill that had seeped into her bones overnight, she had started sweating. She threw off her wrap, but her hands and feet were stone cold, so she wrapped herself up tightly again.

When Gulab came in with her morning cup of tea, she broke out of her reverie and finished packing. She rummaged into her dowry chest for a last look — the chest that her mother had had made with much enthusiasm and hope. Expert carvers had been called, and the best teak wood bought. She sat down to survey what was left of her things — things that she could not take — that purple sari that she had bought with her mother, and the ivory in-laid jewellery box; there was no more room to fit them into the small bag she was taking with her. With unsteady hands, she picked up her cup to sip the tea, but before it could touch her lips, it crashed to the floor.

Gulab, who was tidying her room, rushed to her side. Mira was in tears. "What am I doing?" she cried out in between her sobs. "What will become of me, my parents, Shanti and Kailash?"

Gulab said, "Mistress, this broken glass can only bring you luck. It is a good omen. You must rest now and calm yourself. You have a long journey ahead."

She helped Mira to her bed, covered her with a quilt, and tiptoed out of the room.

After an hour Mira got up to supervise the lunch preparations; she must stick to her routine. She stood in front of the mirror to do up her hair. Her face was white. How would her skin be dark enough to look like Shanti's?

Oh, she had a fever. She felt her forehead; no, it was as cold as the marble statue of lord Krishna at the temple. She looked into the brown pools of her own eyes, and they looked back at her with panic.

But then she stood tall before her image in the mirror, and folded her arms across her chest. She took a deep breath and said to the reflection, "Mira, compose yourself. Be brave and go in peace."

With that, she held her head high, and walked out of her room.

The bustling kitchen preoccupied her for a few moments. When she saw the cook's blackened face and hands, she thought of the herbal powder that Gulab would be applying on her soon. She felt the prickling of tears, and she rubbed her eyes, pretending that it was the smoke from the *chullah* that had made them water.

She served her mother-in-law her lunch, and sat down with her to eat. The bile in her stomach rose to her throat, and she couldn't swallow even a morsel.

"What's the matter, Bahu?" Raj's mother said. "You're going to make me a grandmother soon, I hope."

Mira said, "I'm just tired, Mataji," and escaped to her room.

After lunch, her mother-in-law went to her room to lie down, and the servants were out. Gulab came in to help Mira put on Shanti's clothes and jewellery. She evenly applied the powder to her face, neck, hands and feet. The dark kohl around her eyes made them look large and bright. She really did look like Shanti's sister.

"Mira, Mira! Where are you? Bahu, come here and massage my legs."

Mira and Gulab looked at each other. Mira said, "What shall I do?" Her mother-in-law sometimes came to her room if she did not answer.

Gulab quickly wiped her hands on a towel, and went to the mother-in-law's room, which was open. Even through her closed door, Mira heard Gulab saying, "Mataji, she is fast asleep. Poor thing, she is not feeling well. We should let her nap. I will press your legs for you, if you will allow me."

Then there was silence. But after a minute, Mira jumped up from the bed when she heard her mother-in-law say, "Your hands are so rough. Ouch, you are hurting me! Wake up Mira, or I will get up and go to her myself."

Mira rushed across the room to the dowry chest to try to squeeze herself in, but then she heard Gulab say, "See, this is better, isn't it? I think, you will be getting some auspicious news soon ... we must let her rest." In her anxiety, Gulab must have pressed too hard for her mother-in-law's thick flabby calves.

Why is it taking so long for her to fall asleep, Mira wondered, pacing the length of her room. *I must leave*, she thought, and picked up her bag. Surprised at how heavy it was, she put it down. *I have taken so little; how did it get so full?* She picked it up again to leave as soon as Gulab came in, but remembered that she had yet to cover her head with Shanti's scarf, so she put it down again. Quietly, she opened the door a crack to see what was going on. Just then, Gulab came out from her mother-in-law's room. She rushed to her mistress and did up the scarf. Now Mira was ready to leave.

Gulab went all around the house to check that the coast was clear for Mira to leave through the back door. She returned and nodded. Reassured by her mother-in-law's loud snores, Mira, with a quick look around and a squeeze for Gulab's arm, walked out of Raj's home for the last time.

My marriage is over ... it had never begun, she thought, as she tried not to break into a run; she didn't want to draw attention to herself. She took deep breaths, and walked at a brisk but even pace, though her heart was beating fast. Would he rant and rave when he came home to find her gone, or would he be pleased to be rid of her?

She approached the encampment. Her father's house was just around the corner; she could just peek in for a last look at them. No, no. She would break down and never be able to leave. Oh, was that man someone her father knew? She crossed over to the other side of the road to avoid coming face to face with him. Thankfully, he had walked past without noticing her.

Her heart lurched when she thought of what her mother and father would feel. They would first panic, and then mourn for their lost daughter. Her fingers gripped the bag's handle so tightly that her knuckles turned white in spite of the dark powder covering her skin. How would they explain her disappearance to her brother?

At the encampment, they were all waiting for her to arrive. Kailash and Shanti had told their group about Mira's disguise. Some of the Dom looked at her skeptically, while the others smiled warmly, and nodded in sympathy. The horses were well fed and rested. They sensed the excitement in the camp, and were rearing to go. Kailash was busy with last minute preparations. Shanti and Mira sat close together inside the wagon.

Mira took one last look at the land that was her home, and then tried to focus on the image of her parents that would be forever etched in her memory. Tears threatened to spill out, but she was forced to keep them in check, or her dark skin would turn light again. Shanti gave her hand a reassuring squeeze. The wagon moved forward. The other wagons followed Kailash's lead, and they were soon on their way.

Many on-lookers waved goodbye as the eight wagons, all newly furbished, gleamed in the winter sun, their red and green pennants fluttering in the breeze. The horses looked festive, with bright feathers behind their ears, and embroidered fabrics covering their saddles. Someone started strumming a merry tune on an *ektara*, while Shandar, the eldest among them, joined him on his wooden flute. Mira felt a thrill creep up her spine when she heard the music. But though the others waved back, she and Shanti stayed away from the window.

Mira's palms were clammy, but then turned cold since it was freezing inside the wagon without the warmth of the sun. Her eyes were tightly closed, her fists clenched as she prayed. Every prayer in her mind was interrupted by doubts: *What if they search the wagons to make sure that the Dom haven't stolen anything, and they find my jewellery bag, and drag me to the police? What if a guard recognizes me as Raj's wife? After all, his family is well- known ...what if....*

* * *

It was late afternoon when they reached the old city walls, and the light was fading. Since Kailash's wagon was leading the group, a guard shouted to him in a gruff voice, "Stop!"

When they came to a halt, three guards came forward with their flaming torches. Mira's heart sank, and her eyes widened with fear. Shanti put a finger to her lips, and quickly placed the sleeping Syeira in her arms.

The first guard climbed into their wagon and looked around. Mira and Shanti held their breath as the guard went over to the rolled up stack of quilts at the back. The bag of jewels was in the folds of the second one from the bottom.

Mira kept her head lowered, and pretended to look at the baby. From the corners of her eyes, she saw the guard bend over the stack to see if there was anything hidden behind. Not finding anything but some battered pots and pans, he turned and started towards the door.

Mira let out an almost audible sigh of relief, and couldn't wait to see the last of him. But then he abruptly stopped in front of her and said, "Are you travelling with them?" The guard was too close for comfort, staring at her face.

She pulled her scarf further down her forehead. She remembered to use some Dom words, and nodding towards Shanti said, "Yes, I'm her phen. My dom left earlier."

The guard hesitated. Mira held her breath. For what seemed like a long time, he looked at the sleeping child, and then he left.

The wagons made their way out of the city, and picked up speed. Kailash grinned and waved from his driver's seat. Shanti and Mira smiled at one another. Mira softly kissed the baby in her arms, closed her eyes, and refused to look back. Now, she would only look at the road ahead.

Vidya

I CLENCH MY FISTS. It won't be long now. I taste blood as my teeth bite down on my lip. It feels like the wheels of a truck are crushing my stomach to a pulp. Labour pains are a pin-prick compared to this. I have heard myself babbling when the fever is high. A thick fog blankets my mind, cocoons it from the seriousness of my condition. But there are frightening moments of clarity when I see things as they really are. I don't know what I like more.

Kishore and the doctors think I'm sleeping, but I know that they are here. A few days, the white doctor had said. Kishore must have looked like death. I heard the white doctor's voice again. "We are doing all we can for the child-bed fever. She is not responding to penicillin; other antibiotics are still under trial, as you know."

My husband is a doctor. Can he not do *anything* to save me? He has asked an English doctor from Ajmer's largest hospital to treat me. Soon, there will be no English doctors when our country becomes independent. No English teachers, no police. It will be odd to see only people like us. But I won't be there to see it.

Kalindi and Nandita … how will they manage without me? Little Madhu is asleep in her cradle, her long lashes almost touching her pink skin. Oh, I can't get on my back again; I shouldn't have turned to look at her. I breathe hard to straighten myself. Madhu. Sweet as honey. That's the name Kishore had given her, when I was exhausted after a long labour. Another girl, I had thought, and had closed my eyes. Was Kishore disappointed? I will never know what he feels as he raises her on his own.

He must be thinking of a … a second wife. What am I saying? Oh well, I'm only saying it in my mind, since I can't get a single word out. He can't be considering it. Not yet. He will laugh with her, touch her, kiss her. You silly woman, this jealousy is ridiculous; I will have turned to ashes. They will sprinkle me on Ana Sagar lake, or take me to Bombay and drop the urn into the sea.

Stop being morbid. Think of how good it will be for him and for the girls if he … marries … marries again. But Madhu. She will never know me. You are so cruel, God. Ugg, a strange woman in my bed, in my house. Will my girls call her mother? Please, God, please.

I hear a soft click, and I peek from under half-opened eyes. Kishore tiptoes to my bed. As he approaches, I see his gaunt, unshaven face. I should tell him … a nice woman … marry … before I doze off. My tongue is frozen. Hurry, before he leaves, but I can't, I can't. My lips are stuck together with something gooey.

My eyes fly open to look at him, to convey what I am think-ing. But he only touches my forehead, then flinches. It must feel like the hot tiles on the floor of our verandah in the intense summer heat. Then he sits down on the chair next to my bed, sighing. He is picking at the dry skin around his nails. Yes, it is winter in Ajmer.

That first winter when we moved from Bombay, I froze to death until we bought woollens. I wanted to go back. But I was relieved to be away from my father-in-law's gaze filled with lust, from his pretence at being an affectionate father figure.

There is a hammering in my chest like an insistent warning gong, leaving ripples of fear in its wake. What's happening? I am afraid of death; something I have never thought about. I must speak to Kishore, about … no, not death. I am not afraid of that … then what?

God, no. If his parents move to Ajmer to look after the girls, the old man may try to touch them. Kishore must promise that he will not let that happen. I look at him, but his head is drooping on his chest, and he is snoring.

My poor husband. I have caused him so much anguish. But Madhu will fill him with joy, and the grief over my passing will fade away. Don't blame the child, Kishore, I want to tell him. The girls will be angry and may harm Madhu; children can be so cruel. Kalindi must keep an eye on Nandita. There is so much I need to say, but time is running out, as are these moments of thinking … straight. Lord of Death, Yamaraj, give me time. I manage to open my mouth and say, "Kishore". My voice is hoarse. He does not stir. Black out.

The sun streams in through the window, falling softly on my bed. My eyes flutter open, and I see white clouds gliding across a blue sky. For a beautiful moment I imagine myself lying on the clouds, sailing away. But I'm moaning now. There are explosions of pain inside my head and flashes of intense white light behind my closed eyes, like the firecrackers at Diwali.

My mother's face looms in front of me when I open my eyes again. My parents are still here, looking after Kishore and the girls. My mother's eyes are filled with tears as she wipes my face and tucks my hair behind my ears. Her touch brings back memories. The high fever intensifies every sensation, every emotion.

"Beta," she says, and tries to get a few drops of water past my cracked lips.

I am sitting at the dressing table, my mother behind me, combing my hair. "Which ribbon do you want?" she asks. "The red one today?" My sister and little brother peek in to see what is going on. He toddles over and pulls at the ribbon. I feel the sting of cool water going down my throat. My mother sits down on the chair by the bed.

I want to ask, where are my brothers and sisters? They are like my children. I, the eldest, looked after them. My long brown hair oiled and plaited, I am ready for the day. I'm not at school; after class six I had to be at home to help my mother, and my father had to save money for my brother's education. I sit down with my chalk and slate to write. The slate is full, but I don't want to erase it. I pick up a book from the shelf, and am lost in the story of the Buddha.

Too soon, my mother yells, "Vidya, come and help me in the kitchen." How I hate being taken away from my books and my writing. But dutifully, I get up; at sixteen, I am old beyond my years. I need to take care of my illiterate mother, a woman whose home is her whole world.

I make sure that no one erases my slate, because I want to show it to my father when he returns in the evening. It is only a short poem. He will pore over what I have written and say proudly, "Clever girl. You should have been a boy and helped me with our printing business."

I open my eyes and the images from the past are gone. My father is holding my hand in both of his. Where is Kishore? I need to talk to him, I want to yell, but no words come out. My last thought before I sink into sleep is, I can write.

Kishore. When my marriage was fixed up, my parents had not seen him. They had only seen a photograph that his parents had brought when they visited Surat from Bombay to see me. I had asked them how they could decide without even meeting him. My father had said, "His parents have approved of you."

My mother had said, "He is a doctor like his father. He is fair and has light eyes. They have their own clinic."

"But you have not met him", I had said. My mother, exasperated, had left the room.

My father had smiled and had said, "You will be happy, Beta."

A dashing young man, with a twinkle in his eye. It is our engagement ceremony at home in Surat. I glance at him furtively and fall in love right away. After a couple of months, we are in Bombay. Kishore and I take a short walk together, and he promises me a tutor to continue my studies once we are married. Am I smiling? I feel my lips stretching, but it may just be a grimace because of my sore back.

The first year was a happy time. My in-laws were affectionate; Kishore, a caring man I was in love with, and he with me. I had a tutor who brought me a lot of books, and I was in paradise. The nurse brings me a pencil and paper and props me up. But I slide down like a rag doll, and the pencil and paper fall.

My father-in-law retired from the practice, and Kishore took over the clinic. He was away at work for longer hours. His father would come into my room when I was studying, look over my shoulder, and stroke my back in encouragement.

Kalindi is at her desk, her book open, and she is gazing out of the window. She turns around, startled, as she feels a warm hand on her arm. "What are you dreaming about?" her grandfather asks, grinning. But his touch does not feel right.

Another time, his fingers grazed my breasts as he turned a page of the book I was reading. I pushed him away. I feel metal against my teeth, and something thick and warm in my mouth. I push the hand away so hard that the spoon clatters to the floor.

The nurse says, "She just won't eat anything."

I fell into a heap on my bed and cried. I felt dirty. I am trying to get up to take a bath, to scrub myself clean. The nurse is calling for help as she tries to calm me, to get me to lie down. I am still now, but my cheeks are wet. He was my father-in-law; how could I tell anyone? How could I tell Kishore?

The nurse holds my hand, looking at me anxiously. I am breathing fast. Then I gasp for air. If he can molest his daughter-in-law, he can molest his granddaughters. No, no, that won't happen. Kishore won't let it happen. The nurse rubs my arm, and my breathing slows down. After checking my blood pressure, she leaves. "A panic attack," she says to someone at the door.

When I finally told Kishore what was going on, he looked at me in disbelief. He said, "My father? Impossible." For a week we did not speak, and he could not look at his father in the eye.

But then, we talked again. "Why should I lie?" I asked him. He realized that I was not imagining things. He was filled with anger and shame but did not know what to do. He told me to lock our room when I was alone.

It was during this tense time that Kishore was offered a job in Ajmer's new hospital. I was pregnant with our first child. We jumped at the opportunity to get away. What a relief it would be to not have to constantly be on my guard.

We moved here soon after Kalindi was born. And what a happy life we have. Kishore is one of the best doctors in the city. We have a lovely house with a garden, where I tend to a small vegetable patch. Kalindi and Nandita are doing well at school. The older one wants to become a doctor like her father. And now little Madhu ... we were both hoping for a son ... but it's God's will. What will she be?

I beg you, God, don't take me away from all this. And the social work. The women of our neighbourhood are helping the poor. I am the leader, the organizer. The projects will fall apart without me. No, of course not; no one is indispensable. Chisti Saheb, your Sufi teachings have inspired me to be of service to the community. I turn to you now, pleading at your feet.

Is it morning, evening, or the next day? I am still here, breathing. I think I heard Madhu crying. She must be famished; but, where is she? They have taken her away ... away from me. Useless ... can't even feed my baby.

I see Kishore coming in behind the nurse, forehead furrowed, eyes filled with hopelessness.

"The English doctor will be here any minute", she says as she fluffs up my pillows, and tucks in the sheets. It is so trying to be moved even an inch. Then Kishore feels my forehead and throat. I try to meet his eyes, to communicate. But he is staring into space, scared, lost. Waiting for the doctor's verdict.

The doctor looks grave as he examines me. When he pulls down my eyelids, I see red splotches on his white face. His blue eyes are kind. He turns to Kishore and puts his arm around him. As they move away from the bed he says, "I'm afraid, the end is near."

The next time I wake up, will I be in heaven? No, when my eyes open again, it's not heaven. I am shivering, and my teeth are chattering. Kishore's parents are in the room. He must have asked them to come. They look older since I last saw them. But that doesn't mean that it will stop *him* from anything.

Kishore won't let him examine me; he has not seen patients for years. The thought of how he touched my chest and stomach when I was pregnant with Kalindi, under the cover of examining me, revolts me even now. Thank heavens, he is sitting far from my bed.

My mother-in-law is standing near, twisting the ring on her finger. How could she not have known what had gone on under her own roof? He must have misbehaved with house maids, with patients. The spineless woman was scared to confront her husband. Perhaps, she did tell him to stop, but he was unstoppable.

If the truth came out, the world would come crashing down around her, the family shame exposed. And people would say, so what? That is the way it is with men. You have a good life, so stop complaining. She had decided to turn a blind eye. I feel disgust, but pity too. How had she spent a lifetime with this man? What must she have gone through?

But wait. Kishore ... has he? A dull thudding has started in my chest, and my palms are clammy. Lurking beneath the good husband and father, the skilful hardworking doctor, could be ... could be ... a dark side. He has every opportunity to be alone with female patients. This is madness. It is just my feverish mind playing games with me. Of course, he has not. I am sick in both mind and body to think so.

My dearest Kishore, a monster like his father? The same blood, after all. Stop it, this minute. I would have known. He would have been different with me, especially in bed, if he had ever.... How come this thought never arose in my head before now? Because it is not true. I am weak ... worried about my daughters that's why ... why I'm thinking this. The thought fades, then comes back, persisting like an itch.

I am going to throw up. The nurse grabs the steel basin and puts it under my mouth. Kishore gets up and pats my back. I retch and retch and retch. Nothing. My stomach is empty, with hardly a drop of water in it. The only thing it can hold is pain, a shattering of my body that makes me want to die. No ... the children ... I can't.

I want all of us to be together just once with little Madhu in my arms. Kishore is hovering near me. My tongue has lifted, and with lips barely open I tell him, "Bring the girls with Madhu." There are tears in his eyes as he nods and leaves immediately to get our daughters. This man cannot be a demon in disguise.

This will be my last photograph. On the hospital bed with my family around me. I am propped up, kind of, and Kishore has placed Madhu in my lap. My eyes lock on to hers. Who is this stranger I will never get to know? As her green eyes gaze at my face, I realize that I *know* her; I *recognize* her. Is it from the months that I carried her in my womb? I did the others too, but this one is different. Kishore is holding on to her, just in case. This is the only picture she will have of her and me together.

I am so tired. Everyone leaves, except Kishore. He sits holding my hand as I doze off. I wake up with a start. Kishore is still there. But, what? He is weeping over my hand, kissing it, murmuring my name. I have never seen him sob like this. I try to speak. He looks up at me, wiping his eyes on his shirt sleeve.

How can I tell the love of my life everything I want to? How much I enjoyed my life with him; how lucky I was that he let me study, let me take up community work; giving me a freedom that most women do not have. He treated me like a partner, not like someone beneath him, and listened to my thoughts and ideas. It is over now, this partnership. He is alone, unless … unless he loves another … another woman. Can he?

He looks at me with anticipation. He knows I want to say something. When I open my mouth, he bends to hear. "The girls … your father. Not … alone."

He nods, squeezes my hand, and says, "Never that. Don't worry." He kisses my face, his eyes lingering on every inch. I catch the twinkle in his eye as he tries to make me smile. That is the image I want to leave the world with.

But I want to talk to him seriously first. "You must … must marry … soon." I start coughing, then gasp for breath. Kishore moistens my mouth with water. I need to finish what I started saying. "Marry a good woman … take care … of you, the girls … kind …"

He swallows hard to control his tears. He says, "Vidya, my love, I promise to look after our children, to … to marry." He breaks down, sobbing uncontrollably. Let my husband cry to get over this, so that he can be strong to look after my daughters.

I silently ask for his forgiveness, for doubting his integrity even for a moment. I look intently at his face, and into his eyes, so that I can never forget. A memory that I can carry with me from this life to another. We will meet again some-time, somewhere, because our life together here is cut short, left unfinished.

That's it. I have said the most important things. There is nothing more I can do to ease the way for my children. Now it is between me and You, Yamraj. Where are You going to take me? The fear of death grips me now. Someone is strangling me, crushing my head. I struggle with whatever I have left in me and clutch the edge of the cold bed frame for dear life.

My arms are limp by my side. Kishore's hand is covering mine. My breath is shallow, ragged. For the first time in days I am painless. My body feels light, like a petal floating on a river, coursing along to meet the sea. Everyone is crowded around the bed, crying, praying; watching for my last breath. Kalindi's muffled sobs, and Nandita's wails of Ma recede, as I approach the still depths of the ocean.

* * *

Madhu is looking through the contents of a cardboard box, while her mother and sisters have opened a big metal suitcase and are unwrapping saris covered in muslin. Kalindi is getting married, and they want to see if any of the saris can be used for her wedding.

"Whose saris are those, Ma? Are they yours?"

"No, Madhu, they belonged to Mohti Ma."

"That's her, isn't it?" Madhu is pointing to a framed photograph on the wall above the diwan.

"Yes, Madhu," Nandita said. "She died a week after you were born."

"Is there no other picture of her? I want to know what she was like. She was my real mother."

"Shhh, your real mother is Ma. She brought you up; she is looking after us all," Kalindi said.

Ma said, "Of course, Beta, you want to know. She is your birth mother, after all. Let me see if I can find another photo. I know there is one of all of you together."

Tucked away in the cardboard box, Ma found the photograph in an envelope. The three girls pored over it. Nandita said, "I haven't seen this in a long time."

Madhu took the photograph from Nandita to get a closer look at her mother holding her in her lap.

"Why did you leave me?" she said.

Ma patted her. "This was taken just a couple of days before she passed away in the hospital. Your father told me that she was keen on a picture of all of you together. As you can see, she was very sick; but Madhu, you look a lot like her. Her name was Vidya."

"I'm glad that she insisted on this picture. I have no memories of her." Ma pulled her youngest towards her and gave her a hug. She smiled and thought, she won't be the youngest anymore.

Vidya would be proud of her baby daughter, who had just turned twelve. She is headstrong, but so clever. She loves her books and is always writing something in a note book that she asked her father to get her. He dotes on her, sometimes a little too much, so that the other two get annoyed.

Yes, she would be happy at how the new mother brought her up. Ma sighed. Perhaps, she thought, in those few moments when Vidya held her, she saw something of herself in Madhu.

Then, gently, she took the photograph from Madhu's hand and put it away in the box.

Acknowledgements

I am deeply grateful to everyone at Inanna Publications, especially to Editor-in-Chief, Luciana Ricciutelli, for publishing this book. A big thank you to Inanna publicist, Renée Knapp, for her warmth and her patient responses to my many questions.

I would also like to thank my dear friend, Ruth Donsky, for taking the time to read all my stories, and for her insightful comments. To Teresa Toten, my mentor and confidante, who urged me to keep writing and submitting my work, my heartfelt appreciation.

My love and gratitude to my husband, Devdatt, for taking this journey with me every step of the way. I could not have done this without him. And to our sons, Sidharth and Rohan, for their encouragement and interest in my work, which unbeknownst to them, they inspired me to create.

Aparna Kaji Shah was born in Mombasa, and grew up in Mumbai. She has a Master's degree in English and Aesthetics from the University of Bombay, and an M. Phil. in English from SNDT University, Mumbai. After she moved to Canada in 1985, she obtained a B.Ed. from the University of Toronto. She and her husband, and their family, have lived for various periods in the UK, India, and Singapore. They returned permanently to Canada in 2013 and continue to live in Toronto. Her fiction and poetry have been included in anthologies. *The Scent of Mogra and Other Stories* is her debut collection of short fiction.